Winner Books are produced by Victor Books and are designed to entertain and instruct young readers in Christian principles. Each book has been approved by specialists in Christian education and children's literature. These books uphold the teachings and principles of the Bible.

Other Winner Books you will enjoy:
Sarah and the Magic Twenty-Fifth, by Margaret Epp
Sarah and the Pelican, by Margaret Epp
Sarah and the Lost Friendship, by Margaret Epp
Danger on the Alaskan Trail (three stories)
Gopher Hole Treasure Hunt, by Ralph Bartholomew
Daddy, Come Home, by Irene Aiken
Patches, by Edith V. Buck
Battle at the Blue Line, by P.C. Fredricks
The Peanut Butter Hamster and Other Animal Tails, edited by Grace Fox Anderson

GRACE FOX ANDERSON is editor of Victor Books' new children's line and publication editor of *Counselor,* Scripture Press' take-home paper for children 9 to 11. She has been in church-related work with children for more than 25 years. Mrs. Anderson received her degree in Christian education from Wheaton College, Wheaton, Ill.

THE
HAIRY
BROWN
ANGEL
and Other Animal Tails

edited by Grace Fox Anderson
illustrated by Darwin Dunham

VICTOR BOOKS

a division of SP Publications, Inc., Wheaton, Illinois
Offices also in Fullerton, California • Whitby, Ontario, Canada • London, England

Stories taken from *Counselor* with permission of Scripture
Press Publications, Inc.

Third printing, 1979

Unless otherwise noted, Scripture quotations are from the
King James Version. Some verses are taken from *The Living
Bible* (LB), © by Tyndale House Publishers, Wheaton, Ill.;
The New Testament in the Language of the People (WMS),
by Charles B. Williams, © 1966 by Edith S. Williams, pub-
lished by Moody Press. All quotations used by permission.

Library of Congress Catalog Card No. 76–45040
ISBN: 0–88207–475–X

VICTOR BOOKS
A division of SP Publications, Inc.
P.O. Box 1825   •   Wheaton, Ill. 60187

CONTENTS

The Hairy Brown Angel   7
Rusty's New Family   13
Gabby Plays Hide and Seek   16
Not Only Sparrows   22
Good-Bye, Chippy   27
Jinx, the Alaskan Husky   33
We Watched Autumn Hatch   40
Unexpected Answer   45
Shep on Trial   51
The Night Calvin Foundered   60
Caring for Your Pet   66
Dumb Dog   68
Betty's Shadow   73
Animal Doctor   78
Sarah's Adventure   87
Gary's Guard Dog   94
The Bird that Opens Doors   100
We Remember Baby Robin   105
Ice Break   111
Little Lame Chick   118
Muff   123
Hungry Lions   129

The Hairy Brown Angel

A TRUE STORY by Esther L. Vogt

A cold March rain blew into Mrs. Boyd's face as she stepped from the warm church and sloshed across the lot toward the parsonage.

Pastor Boyd, her husband, had gone to a church meeting in Detroit. Tonight she had attended the women's missionary meeting at church. Since it was late and the children were home alone, she expected the house to be dark. But the kitchen light was still burning.

She let herself in the back door and was surprised to see Ted, her oldest son, studying at the table.

He looked up as she came in. "Hi, Mom. Still raining?"

"Yes, it's a wild night," she said, as she peeled off her wet coat and scarf.

Ted returned to his homework.

Suddenly Mrs. Boyd noticed the huge brown dog lying stretched out beside Ted.

"Ted! What's Browny doing in the house?" she demanded. "He's never stayed inside before!"

Ted glanced up from his book and shrugged. "Oh, he just wanted in, so I let him in. And I decided to do my homework down here and keep him company."

Browny wanted in! That seemed unbelievable. Why, Browny never wanted in!

Of course, everything about the dog was unbelievable. Brown and black and smelly, he was a mixed breed. He had wandered to the parsonage one day and just decided to stay. He adopted the pastor's family and was fiercely protective of them all.

As for coming into the house, he *wanted* to come in. But as soon as he was in, he almost tore the house apart because he was frantic to get *out*. No amount of bribing or petting could persuade Browny to stay indoors even during the wildest weather.

Until now.

There he lay, stretched out calmly in the kitchen like a very ordinary house dog!

Ordinary? Well, not quite. Because of his strange behavior, the family had tried for weeks to get rid of him. He had begun to snarl at children who crossed the parsonage yard on their way to school.

A neighbor, who had always come through with his lunchbox, was forced to walk another way to work because of the dog. More than once the milkman had fought off Browny.

Browny had always come when Mrs. Boyd called

him away from bothering people. Still, there was the danger that someday he wouldn't.

Mrs. Boyd had called the police and asked if they would take care of Browny.

"Sure. We'll shoot him," the captain said. Of course she didn't want that.

The Humane Society had promised to get him if the Boyds would catch the dog and shut him up for them. Shut up Browny? Impossible! Browny wouldn't let himself be penned up *any place!*

That's how things stood that wild, stormy night when Mrs. Boyd came home from the women's meeting at church.

Shaking her head over Browny's strange behavior, she went down to the basement. She bolted the door that led outside, turned down the furnace, then came back up and went into the living room to read the paper. When Ted went upstairs to bed, she decided to do the same. The dog still lay on the kitchen floor, his shaggy head resting on his front paws.

"Maybe I'd better put him out before I go to bed," she decided as she went into the kitchen to lock the back door. Rain still drummed wildly against the windows.

When she tried to get the dog out, he refused to budge. She begged and coaxed and pushed and pulled. He wouldn't move.

She went to the refrigerator for a chunk of meat and tried to lure him to the door. Still he refused to move.

She picked up his hind legs and dragged him out. Like quicksilver, his front end slid back in. She

grabbed his front end, and the back was in. His four shaggy feet seemed like a dozen! No matter how hard she tried, the dog refused to leave the house.

Deciding to shut all the doors to the kitchen and leave the dog inside, she went wearily up to bed.

The next morning the dog was his usual self. He tore frantically from window to door, scratching to get out.

Mrs. Boyd frowned at his strange behavior and went down to the basement to turn on the furnace. What had made Browny so determined to stay in the house last night? She couldn't imagine.

When she reached the bottom of the basement stairs, a gust of damp, cold air blew into her face. A queer, uneasy feeling slithered down her spine. *The basement door was open!* Was—was someone in the basement?

Suddenly she knew. *Someone had gone out of the basement!*

Weak and shaken, she looked around. The basement windows were as snug and tight as ever. Whoever had gone out of that door had been down there last night when she had bolted the door! Whoever it was must have heard her unsuccessful attempts to put the dog out. He knew he had to come up through the kitchen and face the dog or go out the way he had come in earlier—through the outside door to the basement.

That stubborn, smelly pooch had known there was a stranger in the house. God had used him to keep the Boyd family safe!

God has a special job for His angels. Hebrews 1:14

says, "Are they [angels] not all ministering spirits, sent forth to minister for [care for the needs of] them who shall be heirs of salvation?"

God's "ministering angel" had a peculiar form that wild, stormy night. Instead of glorious, dazzling wings, the Lord had given the Boyds' guardian angel four stubborn feet!

Real names not used.

Rusty's New Family

**A TRUE STORY told by Kevin Peterson
written by Marlys Hisel Peterson**

When I was small, our family—my sister, brother, Mom, Dad, and I—moved from Minnesota to South Dakota.

The house we moved into had been empty for two years. It was empty, that is, except for a family of cats. In less than a year we had far too many cats. Daddy gave all but three of them to farmers who had too many mice.

That meant that each of us kids had a cat or kitten of his own. My brother Donald had a black kitten named Midnight. Brenda had a white kitten called Snowball. I had their white, gray, and orange mother. We all called her Mother Cat.

It was a sad day for us all when Brenda's Snowball was hit by a car. Soon afterward, Midnight disappeared! We couldn't find him anywhere.

We felt a little better when Mom told us that Mother Cat was going to have kittens! They were born one spring night in a box we had fixed for Mother Cat near the back door. Three kittens were just like Mother Cat. One was black and white.

They were only two days old when one of us forgot to close the door tightly. That night a stray cat got in and killed them all. We felt terrible!

Late that same summer Mother Cat had four new kittens! We were afraid something bad might happen to them too.

Mom told us to ask God to help us protect and care for our pets. That night we all prayed and promised each other we'd be very careful about shutting the back door each night.

The very next day the kittens disappeared! *It just couldn't be,* I thought. *Not again; not when we asked God for help!* Donald, Brenda, and I looked everywhere, but we couldn't find the kittens.

"God gives animals instincts so they can better protect their babies," Mom reminded us. "Perhaps Mother Cat moved the kittens to a safer place." But we couldn't imagine where they could be. We were sure Mother Cat had "goofed."

"Why don't you feed Rusty and play with him for a while? Maybe he'll cheer you up," Mom suggested. Rusty was our friendly, rusty-colored little dog. He had legs like a bulldog, a body like a dachshund, and a cute face with floppy ears.

I took some food out to Rusty and Donald brought

fresh water. As we were petting him, who should appear in the doghouse doorway but Mother Cat! With a squeal of joy we lunged for the doghouse and there found the four kittens!

Mother Cat had brought her family to Rusty so he could help her protect them! He did too! He kitten-sat while Mother Cat napped in the sun. When they were old enough, they ate from his food and drank his water!

Rusty still didn't like strange cats but he loved "his" kittens. He'd wash their faces with his tongue. When it was time for them to go to bed or if it rained, he'd bark three short barks. Usually they'd obey him. If they didn't, he'd bark again. And he wouldn't go in until they were all inside!

Now, we didn't expect God to answer our prayers in the way He did. But we didn't doubt at all that He had answered!

Gabby Plays Hide and Seek

A TRUE STORY by Doris Steinmetz

"Hi, Mom, I'm home!" nine-year-old Danny shouted. He slammed the door and tossed his school books on the table.

Mrs. Taylor looked up from the pie crust she was rolling out. "Danny, I've told you a hundred times—"

The grin faded from Danny's freckled face. "Aw, Mom, I'm sorry about the door," he said mournfully. "I just get excited and forget."

Mrs. Taylor sighed. "What am I going to do with you, Danny? You'd forget your head if it weren't attached."

Danny slipped out of his jacket and threw it on a chair.

"Hi, Gabby," he called to the bright green parakeet. Gabby chirped a noisy greeting from his cage. "Want

16

to get out a while?" Danny opened the door and the parakeet flew to his shoulder.

"Danny, what about that jacket?" Mrs. Taylor chided.

"Oh, I forgot." Danny picked up the jacket and went into his room. Gabby chattered cheerfully from his shoulder.

"Don't leave it on your bed, now. Hang it in the closet," Mrs. Taylor called after him.

"OK, Mom, I did," Danny said, coming out of his room. "Didn't I, Gabby?"

"Sure," chirped Gabby, in a tiny voice.

"Hear that, Mom?" Danny grinned. "He knows what I say to him."

Mrs. Taylor smiled, then sighed again. "Danny, look at your hair. And tuck your shirt in your jeans."

Absently, Danny smoothed back his sandy hair and tucked in his shirt.

"Wow, I'm starved!" He headed for the refrigerator and poured himself a glass of milk. Next he made a peanut butter sandwich and sat down at the table to eat.

Gabby flew to the curtain rod and began to whistle.

"Now, don't forget to put that bird back in his cage," his mother warned. "He might fly out when the door is opened."

Danny frowned at the thought. The whole family enjoyed Gabby, but no one liked the bird more than he did. Gabby was usually perched on Danny's head or shoulder when he was in the house.

The phone rang and Mrs. Taylor went to answer it.

About that time, Danny heard a familiar voice outside: "Hey, Danny, come on out."

Danny glanced out of the window. It was Tom Casey, his best friend. He was waiting with his bat and ball. Danny swallowed the last of his sandwich, gulped his milk, and rushed outside.

The boys hurried to the vacant lot next door and started to play ball. At first, Tom and Danny took turns batting, but other boys kept coming. Soon they had a good ball game going.

They'd been playing about an hour when Danny heard his brother Bill calling him. At first, Danny tried to ignore him.

Then Bill shouted, "Danny, you come here, this minute!"

Something about the tone of Bill's voice made Danny uneasy. "Could something be wrong?" he wondered. He dropped the bat and ran home. As he entered the house, Bill, Mom, and his sister Mary looked at him strangely.

"What's up?" he asked.

"Where's Gabby?" Bill asked, glowering at him.

Bill and Mary had missed Gabby as soon as they got home from school.

Danny's heart sank when he looked at the empty cage. Gabby had completely slipped his mind when Tom called. "Isn't he here?" he asked, looking around, fearfully.

Mom, Bill, and Mary just stared at him accusingly.

"I . . . I guess I forgot to put him in his cage," Danny stammered. He felt sick. Where could Gabby be?

"So, you forgot again," Mom scolded, "after I warned you."

"Well, Stupid—" Bill's face was red with anger. "—now you've done it. Gabby probably flew outside when you opened the door."

"How could you be so careless?" Mary demanded, bursting into tears. "Now, we'll never see him again."

"He'll probably die too," Bill accused.

Danny had never felt so bad in his whole life. He gulped, close to tears himself. "Have you looked all over the house?" he asked.

"Just in every room—twice," Bill answered sarcastically.

Mrs. Taylor had an idea. "Maybe, if we put the cage outside, Gabby will come to it."

The scowl disappeared from Bill's face and Mary looked up hopefully. "Yeah," Bill agreed, "let's try. I'll get the stepladder, and we can set the cage on it."

"I'll get some celery and put it in his cage," Mary said, rushing to the refrigerator. "Gabby loves that."

Bill grabbed the cage and they all rushed outside. Danny watched them set up the ladder and put the cage on top. They left the door open.

"Gabby," they called, looking about in the trees and bushes.

Danny turned from the window, brushing tears away. Slowly, he went to his room and knelt by his bed. "Dear Lord," he prayed, "forgive me for being careless and letting Gabby get lost. Please help me find him, Lord. I'll never forget again, honest. Please, Lord."

Danny heard a little cry from the doorway. Mom had come in and heard his earnest prayer. She rushed over and took Danny in her arms. "Never mind, Son," she comforted. "It was my fault too. I forgot Gabby myself."

Just then she noticed the half-open closet door. She jumped up and threw the door open wide. There, sitting on the closet shelf, quiet as a mouse, was Gabby.

"Look, Danny," Mom cried. "Gabby, you naughty bird, hiding like that and scaring us all."

Weak with relief, Danny rushed to the closet. Sure enough, Gabby was there, peering out at him and looking as if he knew how much excitement he'd caused.

After Gabby was restored to his cage, they all gathered around and watched him peck at the celery.

Suddenly, Mary noticed that Danny wasn't joining in the happy talk. "Danny," she said, "I'm sorry I was so hateful to you. It was just . . . I was so worried about Gabby."

"Yeah, I guess I was a little rough on you too," Bill admitted. "Watch it, though, from now on, won't you?"

"Don't worry, I've learned my lesson," Danny said.

"Boy, weren't we lucky he was safe?" Bill exulted.

"It wasn't luck," Danny said soberly. "I asked God to help me find Gabby, and He answered my prayer."

Not Only Sparrows

A TRUE STORY by Sara R. Balint

Chippy was gone! Just like that! He had simply disappeared. The ground was dusty and dry, so he didn't leave one little footprint behind.

Chippy, the Thomas Balints' pet turtle, had been put out in the backyard of their home in Westchester, Ill. for exercise. (You'd be stiff too if you spent most of your life in a plastic tub.) It was right after everyone had rushed inside for ice cream and then gone back out that they had missed him.

He wasn't very big. But then Chippy wasn't very small either—just about the size of a baseball. He could have slipped under their white picket fence so easily and headed for who-knows-where!

Chippy knew his name. He would turn his head when any of the seven Balints called. But since he couldn't answer, how would they find him?

Ricky had packed him and brought him home from camp one summer. Now their pet turtle had been with them two years.

Chippy liked to stand on his back legs on the highest rock in his tub-home and peek over the edge. When he got to know the twins, Susan and Marlene, he started taking food right from their hands.

He loved raw hamburger and worms. Always before swallowing, he would slide under water and have a drink. Mother explained that he did this naturally because that was the way God had made him.

But where was Chippy now? The family had covered every inch of sidewalk and curb. They had looked under and around every bush and flower in their yard and their neighbor's. Finally Dad said, "Chippy can smell water even from a distance. He might have headed for the creek." So Ricky dashed down to the nearby creek. However, he returned with a heavy heart and nothing more.

Linda, 10, brushed the tears quickly from her eyes as she searched in back of the garage. No doubt she was remembering how Chippy would stick his head out of the water when she practiced the piano. He'd hold his head to one side, as if he were really listening! At least *he* enjoyed her playing!—or so it seemed.

Her long ponytail bobbing, 4-year-old Cheri trudged along copying the others. She stooped to look under each bush calling, "Chippy, Chippy."

Mr. Balint decided to look in the street sewer for Chippy. "Dad, do you *really* think he could be down

there?" asked Ricky hopefully as he helped his father drag the iron grating off the sewer.

"We'd better look, just in case," his father answered.

But hope turned quickly to disappointment. Their flashlight's beam showed no bobbing little head—only deep, dark water.

"Boy, if we don't find him, I'm never going to camp again," moaned Ricky to the twins. "I'd be reminded of Chippy. I wouldn't have any fun."

Darkness came quickly, making it impossible for

the Balints to continue their search. The five children were tearful as they came in.

Later, they crowded around Mom and Dad for a goodnight kiss. Mom said, "Children, you know the Bible says that God loves us and cares about *all* our problems, big or little. Right now Chippy is our big-little problem.

"God cares for the little sparrows and sees when one of them falls," she went on. "Don't you think He's watching Chippy too? The Lord knows how much he means to us. When you pray about Chippy, remember to thank the Lord for His care. He says in Philippians 4:6, LB, 'Don't worry about anything; instead, pray about everything; tell God your needs and don't forget to thank Him for His answers.'"

"However," Dad added, "sometimes God doesn't choose to answer our prayers the way we'd like Him to. When you pray, ask Him to help you trust Him whether you find Chippy or not."

The children nodded and with very sober faces, climbed the stairs. That night tearful prayers for Chippy's return went up from each bedside while Dad quickly rechecked the backyard with a flashlight.

Returning empty-handed, he shook his head. "You know Chippy really shouldn't be out of water for more than 24 hours," he said sadly to Mother. "He's been gone about five already!"

No call from Mother was needed to bring the twins rushing downstairs next morning. But to their disappointment, Ricky, Cheri, and Linda were already eating breakfast.

"Aw, we thought we'd beat you," they chorused.

"That's not important," answered Ricky. "What really *does* matter is Chippy. The sooner you finish breakfast the sooner we can start looking again!"

Mr. Falson, their next-door neighbor, was outside weeding his flower bed. He waved as they ran out a short time later.

"Understand you lost Chippy last night," he sympathized. "That's tough! He sure was a cute little fellow. If he were mine I would have tied him to a tree by one of his back legs. Then he could have walked around and would not have wandered away." With that he bent down and continued weeding.

Ricky and Linda were halfway across the street when Mr. Falson shouted, "Say now, kids!" Turning, they walked back politely to where he was still bent over. They hated to waste time just visiting.

"Would this maybe make up for Chippy?" he offered as Cheri and the twins came running too. When he straightened up, he had a twinkle in his eye and a turtle in his hand. It was a turtle about the size of a baseball! "Seems he spent the night under one of my pine trees here."

"Chippy!" they all screamed, crowding around Mr. Falson. A few minutes later Chippy was back in his tub with a nice fat worm to make up for his all-night ordeal.

Gratitude to the Lord showed on each happy face as the Balints gathered around him. Truly God had answered prayer and showed them that He loved not only sparrows, but turtles too.

Good-Bye, Chippy

**A TRUE STORY told by Cheri Balint
written by Sally Balint**

Chippy our pet turtle had to go! "It's not as if we're kicking him out," Mom and Dad tried to reason with us. "It's for his own good!"

But you don't just shove a member of your family out! And Chippy had been a part of our family ever since my big brother Rick brought him home from camp a few summers before.

Anyway, what started all this talk about Chippy leaving was the awful sore on his soft-shelled stomach. I think the sore started when he scraped his stomach climbing onto the big rock in the middle of his plastic tub. The sore was so tiny at first we hardly noticed it. But it grew bigger and bigger.

My sister Susie had a good idea! "Why not take Chippy to the vet like people take other animals when

27

they're sick?" My parents agreed. They thought Chippy was special too!

Mom called the vet, and soon she and I were on our way with Chippy between us. We had him in his traveling case—a shoe box with holes punched in the cover so he could breathe.

The doctor was kind and sympathetic. "A pretty big turtle you have here," he said, taking Chippy from me. He turned Chippy over and his smile got smaller. He gently cleaned the sore with antiseptic, then looked at us seriously.

"I'm really sorry." He patted my hand. "I can't tell at the moment if this ulcerated sore has spread yet to his vital organs, like his heart and lungs, you know."

"But can't you give him a shot?" I begged. Much as I hated shots, I knew they were necessary sometimes.

The doctor looked down at me. "I *am* sorry, but some turtles have died just from the shock of an injection. We don't want to take that chance with Chippy." He picked up a bottle of some dark liquid he had been stirring.

"Here is some medicine that *might* start his soft shell growing again." Then he added quietly, "If it's not too late.

"Try to give him three drops a day. Keep his mouth open by putting a toothpick crosswise in it, not up and down, of course. That could hurt him. Also, put 10 drops in his water every time you change it."

The doctor walked out of the office with us. I could tell he was trying to cheer me up. He smilingly said, "I'll expect to see you here in a couple of months with

Chippy. Now take good care of him."

Neither Mom nor I said much on the way home, but Chippy was as excited as ever. He stood up on his little hind legs and tried to push the cover off his box so he could see what was going on.

We ended up putting drops in his water that first night. Chippy just wouldn't let us get near him. He kept swimming around in circles and wouldn't even take food.

Once in a while after that we were able to get Chippy to accept bits of hamburger—his favorite food —with medicine drops on it. Usually we just put the drops in his water.

Finally Dad called us all together. "We have to face this, kids," he began. "Chippy isn't getting any better. Every time he climbs on or off his rock he scrapes his sore, making it worse. Your mother and I have talked about it. We feel Chippy would be much happier if he were back in his natural environment—a lake or creek or river.

"Too, maybe the fresh flowing water would heal his sore. He could live for years yet! Of course we'll all miss him, but when you love someone, including a pet, you want what's best for him. Isn't that right?"

We nodded our heads sadly. I couldn't help remembering the time Chippy got lost and we all prayed for him. God helped us find him again. This time it didn't seem as if God would answer our prayers the way we hoped He would.

One Sunday afternoon in early fall, we drove two miles from our home in Westchester, Ill. to a forest preserve. The seven of us tramped single file through long grass till we reached the woods and creek.

It was cool in the woods. We set Chippy's box down on the muddy bank of Salt Creek and took off the cover. I set Chippy on the ground.

He lifted his little head, sniffed the damp air, then headed straight for the water. He splashed in and a few minutes later we saw him, head held high, swimming downstream.

I couldn't watch too long because tears filled my eyes. Then one of my sisters yelled and I looked and saw Chippy heading back toward shore. He came out on the bank and began pulling long skinny worms out of the mud, one after another. He went back underwater with each one, to help him swallow.

"Sixteen, seventeen, eighteen worms!" we counted. Boy, our turtle was smart! We knew then that we wouldn't have to worry about Chippy going hungry. But one thing still bothered me. Where, in this wide creek, would he find a place to rest when he was tired?

Chippy had disappeared under the water again. Even though he had eaten, nobody wanted to leave. We finally saw him reappear and climb onto an old log that was partly out of the water. He lay there sunning himself for a while. We ran alongside the creek, and when he saw us he swam back to shore again.

Suddenly a large white dog raced out of the woods, barking furiously. With a splash, Chippy dove underwater and swam away. That seemed to be the final proof we needed. Living with people hadn't robbed him of his natural ability to take care of himself. Chippy would be OK.

Slowly we walked back to the car. With a sad heart, I sent up a prayer for Chippy's safety. But mixed in with the sad feeling was a new feeling. It was a good feeling. I was beginning to see how important it was to put the happiness and comfort of others—even of a pet—before my own happiness.

Before I climbed into the car with the rest of the family, I whispered, "Good-bye, Chippy."

Jinx, The Alaskan Husky

A FICTION STORY by Roswell B. Rohde

It happened so suddenly that Jack and his father could hardly believe it. One minute they were mushing steadily northward over the frozen Alaska snow. The next, their huskies were rolling in a tangled, snarling mass of fur and snapping jaws.

Suddenly one of the dogs gave a frightened, agonized yelp. Jack paled. It was Jinx, his favorite husky. The team had attacked him!

Man and boy waded into the middle of the fighting dogs. They struck out right and left with their soft, sealskin boots. Finally they separated Jinx from the other huskies and dragged him back to the sled.

Mr. Dahlman sighed. "This has happened too often, Jack. I don't know what we're going to do about this dog. I'd hate to let him loose to starve in this snow, but we can't go on like this much longer.

"The other huskies are jealous of Jinx. They just won't have a pet on the team. Yet if we don't have teamwork from the dogs, we may never make it to the Barren Lands."

It was the time of year when night lasted 18 out of every 24 hours. Soon it would be completely dark for

six long months. That was the time of storms. The Eskimos called it *Bukera Kuluk* or the time of waiting. Jack and his missionary father had to reach the Barren Lands before then.

During the summer, the Eskimos moved about, searching for food. They gathered berries and preserved them in seal oil. They hunted for meat which they dried and saved for the long winter months Reaching them with the Gospel in the summer was hard because they were too busy to sit and listen or study.

But during the time of the long night, the Eskimos stayed in one place. Mr. Dahlman could then go and visit them for several weeks. He had time to teach them about Jesus and His great love. Even now Ayukka and his people would be preparing for their arrival. Ayukka was a new believer and their friend.

Mr. Dahlman had not planned to go north with only his 14-year-old son Jack to help. But Kogema, his guide, was suffering from a foot infection and unable to walk.

No one else had been willing or able to make the long journey. Finally the missionary and his son set out alone. But despite the constant dangers, they had had a good trip so far. Good, that is, except for the problem with Jinx.

Jack sighed. *Jinx!* They had raised all the huskies. He had petted and played with all the dogs. But none of them had responded as Jinx did, so Jinx had become his favorite. And yet this beautiful dog seemed born to trouble as his name suggested.

Jack patted the quivering dog. Fortunately, only the animal's pride was hurt. Suddenly Jack had an idea. "Maybe Jinx wants to be the leader, Dad!" he cried. "Why don't you give him a try?"

Mr. Dahlman thoughtfully tugged at the frost-tipped fur of his parka. "Well, I guess he's smart enough. At least if he keeps ahead of the others, he'll be safe. And they'll pull hard to keep up, that's for sure. OK, let's move the lead dog back. I don't think he'll fuss too much."

After repairing the harness and rehitching the dogs, they were off again. For a time all went well. Each dog jealously tried to keep up with Jinx. And Jinx led well.

"Another day and we'll see Ayukka," the missionary remarked. "He promised to meet us at Point Ordeal."

Jack grinned in the biting wind. "Well, I hope he has a nice fire going when we get there!"

It would be fun to see Ayukka again.

The kind Eskimo had come from the Barren Lands some months before. He had stayed at the Dahlmans' mission for a couple of weeks just to hear about Jesus.

After he had received Christ as his Saviour, Ayukka had asked the missionary to help him tell his people the Good News. Mr. Dahlman had promised to come before the long night set in. Now he and Jack were almost there.

Jack looked up. Funny he hadn't noticed before, but the wind had become much stronger. Spits of snow and ice stung his face.

"Looks like a blizzard, Jack," his father shouted over

the roar of rushing wind. "It may strike at any minute. We don't dare lose any time."

The dogs seemed to sense the urgency. Jinx strained at his harness. But the wind was so strong that it was like trying to push into a solid wall.

Jack prayed as he never had before: "Dear Lord," his heart cried, "help us reach Point Ordeal safely. We may not have a chance to share the Bible message with this group of people again."

Suddenly Jinx swung out to miss a deep crack in the icy snow. But the other dogs didn't see it in time and kept coming. One sled runner caught in the crack and the dogs piled up in a yelping mass. The sled tipped over, spilling its contents and the men into the stormy night.

Battling the biting snow, Jack and his father picked themselves up, then untangled the dogs. "Hey," Jack cried, looking around. "Where's Jinx?" He called and called, but there was no sign of the dog. He had run away, deserted!

Now all they could do was huddle with their huskies against the upset sled. They would have to wait for the blizzard to stop before they could reload. It could be a long wait. Such winds often blew for 10 days or more. And just *one night* sitting still in merciless wind and cold—60-80° below zero—could mean death.

Mr. Dahlman drew his son's head near his own. "O Lord," he prayed, "we believe it is Your plan for us to take Your Word to these people. If so, then please help us go on. If not, then Father, 'to die is gain,' for it only means being with You forever."

Several miserable hours passed. Gradually, the wind began to die down. They could see twinkling stars again. Father and son got up stiffly and began mending the broken harness. They righted the sled, reloaded it, and hitched up the huskies, putting in another lead dog.

Mr. Dahlman got behind the sled, took hold of its handles, then gasped. "Jack!" he said, "look what the wind has done. Nothing looks the same!"

It was true. The wind and drifting snow had blotted out their trail and all landmarks. Even with a compass they might miss Point Ordeal by many miles.

Suddenly they heard a noisy bark across the dark wasteland. "Jinx!" Jack cried.

The dog hurled through the air, into his arms, and both landed in a drift. "Jinx," Jack murmured happily, "I knew you'd come back!"

A call came, then, through the night and the figure of a man appeared. "Ayukka!" cried Jack and Mr. Dahlman together.

They greeted each other warmly. "The dog came to me in the darkness," Ayukka explained. "I knew him from my weeks with you. I fed him and tried to get him to rest. But he insisted on leading me back to you."

Mr. Dahlman scratched the dog's ear affectionately. "Jinx," he said, "we thought you had deserted us. But God used you to answer our prayers!"

The missionary reached down and unhitched the other lead dog. "Move over, Pepa," he said kindly. "Jinx will lead this team from now on!"

We Watched
Autumn Hatch

**A TRUE STORY told by Mary Sue
and Martha Lou Adair
written by James R. Adair**

It may seem strange, but our "Autumn" adventure started on a spring day when we decided to sell seeds.

One of the premiums in the seed catalog was a Chick-U-Bator. We thought it would be fun to watch chickens hatch. So when we had sold our 42 seed packets, we sent in the money and asked for the Chick-U-Bator. Then we waited.

One day after school in early June, our small incubator arrived. Now all we needed were the eggs. The booklet with the Chick-U-Bator said that we needed fertile eggs—eggs laid by a hen with a "husband."

Daddy got eggs from a farmer. We carefully followed directions as we set up our incubator. Then we placed two eggs in the incubator and turned them three times a day. (If you've watched a mother hen, you know she reaches under her body and turns her eggs with her beak.)

Our booklet said the eggs must be turned till the 18th day. Turning them prevents the embryo (M-bree-O) or growing chick from breaking through the white and being squeezed to death against the shell.

Our family talked a lot about the miracle we thought was going on in the eggs. Miracle is a good word for it. Only God can put life in an egg!

We even prayed that God would help our eggs hatch. In Sunday School we had learned that God is interested in all His creation, and eggs are part of what He made.

But our first egg-hatching experiment failed! The 21st day came and went without any sign of life. After about 23 days, we broke the eggs open. One had nothing in it except yolk and white. The other contained a dead embryo with feathers.

We tried a second time and again we failed. But we didn't give up. We stopped at a farm and a nice lady gave us two Bantam chicken eggs. She said they would hatch in about 19 days. (Bantams are dwarf chickens. They hatch faster than larger chickens.)

We put the Chick-U-Bator on Daddy's desk, away from the sun. We watched the temperature and water and turned the eggs very carefully.

Summer passed and school began again. We counted the days and prayed. The 19th day came and went. Not a peep from the eggs. (Our booklet said that the chick begins to peep about 20 hours before it pecks its way out of the shell.)

It looked as if our third try was a failure too. Then early the 20th day, September 22, Martha Lou went downstairs to look at the eggs. "I heard it peeping!" she cried, running upstairs.

At lunchtime we checked the eggs again. "There's a crack in one of the eggs!" we squealed together. Everyone gathered around. A ragged little crack near the large end told us that the miracle of birth would soon occur before our eyes.

Our booklet said the chick would have to peck a circle clear around the large end of the egg. What a job for such a little fellow!

Well, we ate our lunch, went to school, and then ran all the way home that afternoon. Out of breath, we saw that the crack was bigger. So we sat down to watch.

Then something scary happened. Mary Sue accidentally tipped the incubator, spilling both eggs! One egg dropped on the floor and, splash! Raw egg went all over.

To our relief, there was no chick in that egg. The other egg—the cracked one—rolled onto Daddy's desk and didn't break. Our hearts were in our mouths!

After we cleaned up the mess and put the cracked egg back in the incubator, Mary Sue burst into tears. Fearfully, we continued our watch. Had the fall hurt the chick?

Suddenly the egg began to wiggle and crack again. He was OK! Imagine our relief.

About an hour after the near tragedy, the chick gave a big heave and burst the shell open. Out he tumbled— wet, ugly, and tired.

As he grew stronger, he wobbled around the incubator. Daddy said he had hatched just as autumn officially came—about 5:40 o'clock. So we named our chick Autumn.

And the name fit our little Bantam perfectly. He wasn't like any chick we had ever seen. He was reddish-brown, a real autumn color. In a few hours, little Autumn was walking and pecking at his shell.

The next day, we put him in a box where we could keep the temperature just right. We fed him ground corn.

Our friends enjoyed Autumn too. Some came to see him just after he hatched. Another friend, Janet De-Vries, chick-sat one weekend while we were gone. We even took Autumn to school.

We kept him for several months. When he began waking us up every morning, crowing, we had to give him to a farmer friend. It was hard for us but best for him.

But we'll always remember watching Autumn hatch. Seeing the miracle of a little chick break out of an egg, made us realize more than ever what a great God we have. A song we like sums up our feelings:

"All that our mighty God hath made,
Mountain and sky and sea,
Blossom and tree and living creature,
He gave me eyes to see.
Great and marvelous are His works,
Great and marvelous are His works,
A mighty Creator is He!" *

---

* "Our Mighty Creator," © 1949, Scripture Press.

Unexpected Answer

A FICTION STORY by Marie Chapman

Debbie Ralston sat by her front window, watching her friends come home from school. Several of them waved and smiled. Debbie waved, but it was hard not to cry.

Just after Christmas, she had awakened with a fever and sore throat that kept getting worse. Finally she had to spend almost three weeks in the hospital. Even after she had come home, she had to stay in bed a lot and tired easily.

Last week the doctor came to see her. He took her pulse and listened to her heart and asked questions while her parents stood by.

Finally he smiled and said, "You're doing well, young lady, but we want to be real sure. Your mother tells me you're keeping up your studies at home, so let's just postpone your schooling till next fall."

Then he went out into the hall and spoke to Daddy: "She'll be all right," Debbie overheard him say, "but she needs a long rest. Keep her quiet this spring and summer."

"That means no church camp this summer," Debbie groaned. She leaned back, tears running down her face.

Mother put her arms around her.

"For a whole half year I can't do anything," Debbie sobbed.

"I don't think you realize what a sick girl you've been," Mother said. "Daddy and I are grateful the Lord made you better. But let's ask Him to help you be patient. OK?"

A few days later she was sitting in the kitchen with Mother. "Mom, do you think the Lord hears me about patience? The days seem so long."

Mother was thoughtful. "I'm sure He does. But sometimes He answers in a way we're not expecting. We'll just keep praying about it."

Mother wiped off the kitchen table, then straightened up suddenly. "Debbie, look," she said.

On the windowsill sat the prettiest cat Debbie had ever seen. He was big and fat and glossy black. His feet were spotlessly white. He looked in hopefully, whiskers twitching.

"Oh, Mother, let him in!" begged Debbie.

Mother laughed and went to the door, calling, "Kitty, Kitty!" She held the door open, and he came in and stood, looking around.

Debbie called, "Here, Kitty." He trotted over to her chair and jumped into her lap.

"Do you suppose he's hungry? Should we fix him some breakfast?" Mother asked.

"Oh, yes, Mother. What would he like?"

Mother put some milk in a pan on the stove and after a minute poured it into an old saucer on the floor. The big black cat was at the saucer in a flash, lapping away in such a hurry that he got milk on his whiskers.

Debbie laughed and laughed. "Mother, can I keep him? Can he stay here? Please, Mother."

Mother hesitated. "Well, Debbie, I'm afraid he's somebody's pet. He's such a pretty cat and so fat and friendly. Someone's been feeding him and playing with him. I think we'd better put him out so he can go home."

Debbie was sad. "Oh, Mother, I can't bear to have him leave."

Mother gently picked the cat up and put him outside. Soon Kitty was back on the windowsill again.

That evening Debbie begged Mother and Dad to bring the cat in.

Mother was worried. "Maybe I shouldn't have fed him. He may not want to leave."

Dad phoned the neighbors to try to locate the owners of the cat but had no success. "We'll have to bring him in," Dad decided. "But in the morning, he must go out, Debbie, understand? We must not keep someone else's pet."

Debbie nodded, only half listening. When the big cat came in, he came straight to her. He jumped onto

her lap—as if he knew Debbie had been waiting for him.

"I'll call you Toby," Debbie decided.

Debbie played with Toby until bedtime. When Mother took off her apron and threw it over a chair, Toby saw the apron strings dangling. He ran over and began batting at the strings. Debbie giggled with delight.

Father watched him play for a while, then left the room. He came back with Mother's yardstick. He had tied a piece of bright red ribbon on the end.

Debbie took it. Toby sat, watching the red ribbon with his big green eyes. She swung the ribbon back and forth and he pounced on it.

When he let the ribbon go, Debbie swung it wide. Toby raced after it, losing his balance and skidding into the sofa. Debbie laughed hard and her parents joined her.

"May I keep him if we can't find his owners?" she begged.

Her parents looked at each other. "Don't plan on it," Mother said. "It's too unlikely."

"Let's just wait and see," Father said.

For two days, they brought Kitty in at night and put him out in the daytime. Most of the day he either sat on the windowsill or took short walks around the house.

Miss Walker, the visiting teacher, came by the house again to help Debbie keep up with her schoolwork.

As she got up to leave, she saw Toby standing by the door. "There's that cat!" she exclaimed.

Mother looked surprised. "Is it your cat, Miss Walker?" she asked.

Miss Walker laughed and started toward the door. "Oh, no," she said. "He doesn't belong to anyone—or he didn't till now. He came to the school right after Christmas. The children fed him and played with him, but no one has seen him recently. He looks as if he likes it here."

That evening Debbie played happily with Toby. She petted him and stroked his thick fur. "You're really mine," she told him.

Next morning while Debbie was eating her breakfast and Toby was lapping his milk, Debbie had a sudden thought. "Mother, you said the Lord sometimes answers prayers in ways we don't expect. Do you think maybe He sent Toby to help me be patient?"

Mother smiled. "I wouldn't be surprised," she said.

Debbie sat and thought.

"I'm sure He did," she said at last. "I'm going to thank Him for Toby and for answering my prayers in a way that was nicer than anything I would have asked for."

Shep on Trial

A FICTION STORY
by Dorothy Grunbock Johnston

Shep bounded up as Barney Jorden picked up a pail and scoop. Every day when the tide went out, Barney went clam digging and Shep tagged along.

Not that Barney liked clams that well himself. But the summer people from the city did. Clams weighed heavy and they paid him by the pound. Barney needed all the money he could earn.

He was the man of the family while Dad was laid up. Dad said he'd be as good as new when he was up again. But right now he was in a hospital bed on their wide, enclosed porch. Mr. Jorden wouldn't be able to get back to his job at the mill until his back got better. The doctor said it would be several weeks yet.

Barney earned what he could by digging clams and picking raspberries. True, his dad got a regular insur-

51

ance check, but Mom said it didn't always stretch to cover their needs.

Shep raced along the tideflats, exploring at the water's edge. Having Shep along made the work seem more like fun. The big collie ran up to him, and Barney ruffled the fur behind the dog's ears.

"I'm sure glad I've got you for company, Shep," he said. "You're the best dog ever."

Barney searched in the wet sand for a place where small bubbles appeared—sure signs of a clam burrowing into the sand. "Here's one!" he cried and began to dig fast with his scoop. About 10 inches down, he

found one and dropped it into the bucket. It was always fun at first, digging up the clams. But after a while his arms and back got tired.

Sea gulls circled overhead, waiting for him to uncover some bit of food. One landed and waddled down the beach. Shep took off after it, barking furiously. He seemed to like hearing it screech and scold as it flew up out of his reach.

"Here, Shep!" Barney called. "Don't tease the gulls." But he knew the big dog wouldn't hurt them.

When his pail was full, Barney whistled for Shep and started back to the house. They lived on a bluff, just off the wide ocean beach. It was a nice spot. Barney loved the ocean and silently thanked God for their home. He also thanked Him that his dad hadn't been killed when he'd fallen and hurt his back at work. "Things could be a lot worse, Shep," he told his dog.

Back at the house, Barney showed his pailful of clams to his dad. "Barney," Mr. Jorden said, "I lie here and read my Bible and thank the Lord for giving me a boy like you. You and Shep will see us through these lean days. When I get the kinks out of my back, I'll be as good as new."

Barney grinned. "I sure hope so, Dad," he said. "We're going to take these down the shore to the cottagers. I'll be back in time for lunch."

He picked up the pail again and Shep hurried after him. On the way, they passed old Mr. Menche's place. The old man lived there the year round like the Jordens. Mr. Menche had retired. He had a garden and kept some chickens and sold the eggs to the summer

people. He was out in his garden when Barney and Shep passed.

"Hi, Mr. Menche," Barney called out.

"Don't you 'hi' me, Barney Jorden," the old man growled as he looked up from his work. "Found eight more baby chicks dead this morning! Mauled to death, they were. Mauled by some dog, I'll swear. And that collie of yours is the only one round here." He spat on the ground.

Barney was surprised. Mr. Menche was always kind of grouchy but he'd never been mean. "B-but, Mr. Menche," he answered. "You know Shep. He wouldn't chase your chickens. I'm sure he didn't kill them."

"You may be sure, but I ain't," the old man replied. "I see your dog chasing them sea gulls. They're birds same as my chickens. I tell you if I lose one more chick, I'll call the sheriff. That's what I'll do. Them chicks is my living."

The old man turned back to his work, and Barney went on his way, puzzled and worried. How could he accuse Shep like that? Barney knew Shep hadn't gotten into Mr. Menche's chickens.

Later, when he got home, he tried to hide his worry from his dad while Mom got lunch. But it was no use.

"What's the matter, Son?" his father asked.

"Oh, Dad," Barney said, sighing. "Old Mr. Menche thinks Shep is killing his chicks. He's real mad. I've never seen him so cross. Says he'll call the sheriff if he finds any more dead. I know Shep didn't do it."

"Come over here, Barney—by my bed," his dad told him. "Let's talk to God about this. You've belonged to Him for about three years now, haven't you? There's nothing too big or too small to tell Him, you know."

Barney nodded, and the two bowed and prayed there beside his dad's bed.

It was a few minutes before 5 the next morning when Barney woke up. He glanced out the window. The tide was high. It lapped at the beached rowboat.

"Why not?" Barney asked himself. In a few minutes he was dressed. He unchained Shep and gathered the things he needed to catch some fish.

"Dad lies there unable to get out. I bet he'd like a nice mess of fish for breakfast," he said to Shep. "Hope he didn't see us. I'd like to surprise him."

They climbed into the boat and Barney pulled on the oars. Small waves slapped at the bow as they headed out around the point into the bay.

Shep lay on the back seat, his head on his paws. A gull screeched overhead. Shep sat up and barked loudly.

"Quiet, Shep," Barney ordered. "I want this to be a surprise!"

Shep lay down again. He was a good dog. Minded real good, Barney thought appreciatively. Mr. Menche should know Shep would never go after his chicks.

By the time the 7 o'clock whistle blew at the mill, Barney had two nice-sized flounder. They'd make a good meal for his parents and him.

As they rowed past Mr. Menche's place, Barney wondered about the chickens. Even if more were dead, the old man couldn't blame his loss on Shep this morning. Shep had been chained all night and out in the boat with him.

Still, if Mr. Menche had it in his head that Shep was to blame and called the sheriff, the sheriff might believe a man rather than a boy. Barney beached the boat and bent over to gather up the fish and tackle.

Shep crowded past him and leaped onto the beach. "Hey, what's your hurry?" Barney asked. Glancing up, he saw Shep streak up the beach. Of all places, he was headed straight for Mr. Menche's!

"Shep!" Barney called. "Shep, come back here!"

But the dog acted as if he hadn't heard.

"Shep! Here, boy. Shep, come here!"

Barney's heart beat a loud tattoo. Shep always obeyed him. Why wouldn't he come now? If the old man saw Shep, it would be just too bad.

And suddenly there he was, standing at his door. "You come here, Barney Jorden!" Mr. Menche called out angrily.

Barney walked slowly up to the old frame cottage.

"What did I tell you?" Mr. Menche stormed. "I just counted five more dead chicks. And that brown cur of yours just streaked past me into the woods. Don't you deny it. I'm calling the sheriff now."

Barney sent up a hasty prayer. Shep hadn't killed the chickens, he knew. But how could he prove it? Again, he called Shep, but the dog didn't come. He trudged slowly home, all the joy of the morning gone.

Mom and Dad were thrilled with the fresh fish for breakfast, but Barney couldn't enjoy his. Why had Shep dashed off for the Menche's place? Why wouldn't he come when Barney called?

A little later there was a knock on the porch door. Barney was drying dishes for his mom. He glanced out the window and saw Mr. Menche. Did he have the sheriff with him? Barney walked to the kitchen door and listened. Why, the old man was laughing.

"Guess I got to apologize," he was saying. "Just a while ago I saw that dog of Barney's come out of the woods. He had something in his mouth. I was sure it was one of my chickens. But when I went outside to see, the joke was on me. A weasel, it was. Biggest weasel I ever did see. And you know I've lived here near 50 years now. Yes, sir, that weasel must have killed my chicks—13 of them. And here I was blaming that dog."

Barney stepped outside. Shep jumped up and licked his face. Barney hugged his dog. "Hear that, boy?" he said.

"Guess you heard what I told your pa," Mr. Menche said. "Your dog killed the culprit, a great big weasel."

Barney nodded. Shep was a good dog. He knew it and God knew it and now Mr. Menche knew it.

"Hope you don't mind," Mr. Menche was saying. "I gave Shep a big bone. And if you've time, young man, I could use your help in my garden. I'll pay you to weed. It's too much for me this year with my arthritis bothering me the way it is."

Barney grinned. "Sure," he agreed. "If Shep is welcome too. He's good company."

"Just so long as he don't trample the garden," Mr. Menche said. "Wouldn't hurt none to have a watch dog around my chickens once in a while."

The Night Calvin Foundered

**A TRUE STORY told by Mark Houvenagle
written by Shirley Houvenagle**

I put my arms around my gray pony's furry neck and
hugged him tightly. "I'm sorry you hurt so much, Calvin," I told him. He was so sick he had trouble holding up his head. He leaned it on my shoulder and
whinnied softly.

It was late afternoon the year I was 11 when I discovered he was sick. I had gone out and called him,
but he swayed on his feet. He seemed unable to walk.
Usually he came right up to me, looking for the sugar
cube I sometimes carried.

This time he just made sad little rumblings down
in his throat and lowered his head forlornly. I hurried
to the house. "Mom," I called. "Something is wrong
with Calvin. He can hardly walk or hold up his head."

We called Dr. Birchmeir, the vet, and told him that

Calvin was sick. He asked right away if Calvin had gotten into the grain bin. "It sounds as if Calvin has foundered," he added.

My heart nearly stopped. I had just read about founder in a library book on horses. It's a disease every horse owner fears. It's caused by horses over-eating. Corn causes it most often.

I ran to the corncrib to see if Calvin had broken in, but it was locked securely.

The book had said a lot more. Sometimes animals died if they weren't treated promptly. It seems that horses can't belch or vomit to relieve discomfort when they've overeaten. And the trouble in their stomachs effects their feet.

The blood vessels in their feet get stretched and enlarged. This makes the hooves hot and feverish. Their body weight on these sore feet causes bone damage and walking is terribly painful for the horse. The kindest thing its owner can do is have the animal destroyed.

I couldn't bear the thought of destroying Calvin. While living in the city, I had dreamed of having a brown and white pony and a saddle. Calvin was gray with three layers of winter hair and I had no saddle, but I didn't care. He was my very own. That part of my dream had come true.

Dr. Birchmeir said he would come early the next morning and give Calvin shots of cortisone in each leg. However, that night, getting the fever out of Calvin's feet was up to us.

He had said there were several things we could do

that would help Calvin. We could tie some bags of ice on each foot or spray his feet with cold water from the garden hose.

Or we could force Calvin to lie down and stay off his feet or even dig a hole and fill it with cold water and make Calvin stand in it. The main idea was to do something to reduce the swelling and fever so Calvin's feet wouldn't be damaged forever.

Dad had gone to a school board meeting, so Mother and I asked God to help us do the thing that would help Calvin most.

When we were through praying, I ran to get the garden hose. It was too short to reach the spot where Calvin stood, so I carried buckets of water from the end of the hose to him.

It was a cold February evening, but I began to sponge his feet with rags soaked in the water. He jumped and whinnied when I put the cold rags on his feet.

"You're going to be all right, boy," I told him as I worked. "Just stand still." He seemed to know I wanted to help him. He looked at me in the darkness and nuzzled me with his nose.

When Dad came home an hour later, Calvin's front feet had cooled down, but his back ones were still burning with fever. Together, Dad and I began digging a hole near the pasture gate and soaking the ground with water. While we dug, we talked:

"Calvin's overeating," Dad said, "is kind of like people sinning against God. Even if Calvin had known better, he would have done it anyway because he liked what he was doing. Some people are like that, only they understand better than a pony does what the results will be."

I remembered that the Bible says the result of sin is death, but God has a cure. The cure is believing in the Lord Jesus. I felt sorry for people who chose to ignore what God says in His Word.

After we were sure the hole was big enough, we pushed and pulled poor Calvin into the mud. It seemed cruel when he was so sick, but we knew it was best for him.

When we had him in the right spot, Dad built a small fence around him. I held the flashlight while Dad worked.

"I'm going to get some hay for Calvin to munch on, Dad," I said when he had finished the fence. "The vet thought it might help him feel better." And it did cheer the pony a little.

It was nearly midnight before I went to bed, but I lay for a long time thinking about Calvin. I prayed that God would make him well if it was His will.

Only recently our collie named Valley had been killed by a car. I could hardly bear the thought of losing Calvin too.

Next morning, while I was at school, Dr. Birchmeir came and gave Calvin a shot in each leg. When Dad let Calvin out of his pen, he hobbled stiffly away. We wouldn't know for two or three days if the treatment had been successful.

The first day he spent lying down. The second day he wasn't much better. Each day I prayed for him.

The third day was Sunday. I looked out of the bedroom window while I was getting dressed for Sunday School. I could hardly believe my eyes. Calvin was walking slowly along the garden fence! He wasn't even limping! I bowed my head and said, "Thanks, Lord."

Calvin got well and I certainly was grateful. He wasn't quite as sure on his feet as he had been, but we kids could still ride him.

I never did find out what he had eaten, but I did find his hoofprints by the corncrib. We think maybe the rain washed corn out into the grass and Calvin ate that.

Anyway, I'll never forget the night Calvin foundered or the way God answered prayer for him.

CARING FOR YOUR PET

by DR. ROBERT ALLEN and BERT TIEDEMANN

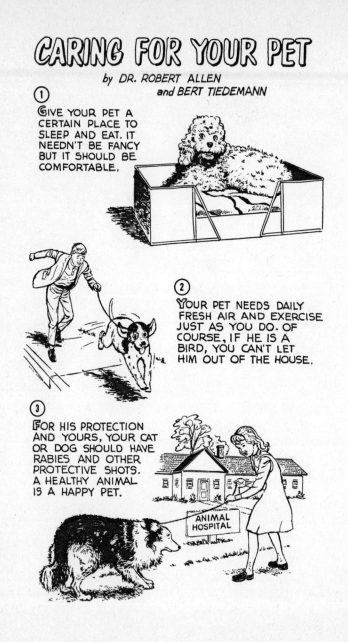

1 GIVE YOUR PET A CERTAIN PLACE TO SLEEP AND EAT. IT NEEDN'T BE FANCY BUT IT SHOULD BE COMFORTABLE.

2 YOUR PET NEEDS DAILY FRESH AIR AND EXERCISE JUST AS YOU DO. OF COURSE, IF HE IS A BIRD, YOU CAN'T LET HIM OUT OF THE HOUSE.

3 FOR HIS PROTECTION AND YOURS, YOUR CAT OR DOG SHOULD HAVE RABIES AND OTHER PROTECTIVE SHOTS. A HEALTHY ANIMAL IS A HAPPY PET.

ANIMAL HOSPITAL

④ BE SURE TO GIVE YOUR PET FRESH WATER EACH DAY. FEED HIM AT A SET TIME.

⑤ BATHS AND GOOD GROOM-ING WILL MAKE YOUR PET PLEASANTER TO HAVE AROUND, ESPECIALLY IF HE IS A HOUSE PET. MOST BIRDS ENJOY SPLASHING IN A BATH OR UNDER THE FAUCET.

⑥ AN OBEDIENT PET IS A JOY TO OWN. DON'T BE AFRAID TO TEACH YOUR DOG OR CAT GOOD MANNERS.

⑦ LAST, BUT NOT LEAST, YOUR PET NEEDS LOVE AND FRIEND-SHIP.

Dumb Dog

A FICTION STORY by Muriel Larson

"Prince, how many times have I told you not to chase cars!" Mark scolded. Prince romped up to Mark, wagging his tail and panting hard.

"Dumb dog," Mark said affectionately, running his hand through Prince's soft collie ruff. "When will you learn to obey me? I don't want you to get hurt."

Prince was a wonderful dog—if only he would obey!

On his way home, Mark met Warren Swift. His dad didn't approve of Warren, but Warren was different from the other guys. Mark felt big when he was with him.

"Say, Warren, I see you got your new sports bike," he said admiringly.

Warren stood at his bicycle. "Yeah," he answered proudly. "And look at all the extras."

Mark examined the dual handbrakes, leopardlike sports seat, and five-speed stick shift. The chrome handlebars and frame glinted in the sunlight. "Wow, it's cool!" he gasped. "It must have cost a fortune!"

Warren shrugged. "My parents get me anything I want," he said. "Would you like to have a ride?"

"Would I!" exclaimed Mark. He could hardly keep from jumping with excitement. Warren got off the bike and handed it to Mark. Mark climbed on carefully and took off! It was like riding on the wind! Prince raced alongside. Bicycles, cars, they were all the same to Prince—great fun to chase!

Mark rode around the block and came up beside Warren just as Warren was nearing Mark's house. Mark skidded to a halt, and Prince did too. "That's a keen bike, Warren," he said. "I hope I can ride it again sometime."

"Sure, any time," said Warren carelessly. "Say, why don't you come over tomorrow after school? I've thought up something real groovy to do." A mean gleam glinted in Warren's eyes, and Mark knew in his heart that Warren had probably thought up another trick that might get him in hot water with neighbors or the law.

Mark didn't want to get mixed up with that side of Warren. But he did enjoy riding his bike, or going fishing in his boat, and things like that.

"Er, maybe some other time, Warren," Mark said. "I'll have a lot of homework tomorrow. See you again soon, though." He waved and walked to his house.

Mark's dad had just come home from work and was

getting out of the car. "Mark," he said sternly, "wasn't that Warren Swift I just saw you with?"

Mark hung his head slightly. "Yes, Dad."

"Well, didn't I tell you not to have anything to do with him?" his dad asked. "You know he's been in trouble with the law. He's wild, and he'll get anyone in trouble who runs with him. When will you learn to obey your mother and me?"

"But, Dad," Mark argued, "Warren isn't as bad as you think he is. He's a lot of fun. He's got a fishing boat and now he has that beautiful new sports bike."

"Son, I know there are a lot of things about that boy that attract you, just as a moving car attracts Prince," his father scolded. "But I want you to obey me and stay away from Warren! Remember, Mark, when you disobey us, you're disobeying God's Word. Now I don't want to have to speak to you about this again!"

Mark's father went into the house, leaving Mark standing and staring sadly at the ground. How much he wanted to ride that bike again!

Mark steered clear of Warren for some time. As a Christian, he wanted to obey his parents and please Christ. But every time he saw Warren riding the bike in the distance, Mark wanted a ride too.

Then one day, when Mark was riding on his old bicycle, Warren came sailing along on his new one. He coasted up to Mark. "Say," he asked, "have you ever tried going down Hill Street on a new sports bike?"

Mark grunted. "I've never even tried it on an old bike. That street is too dangerous. Broad Street, with all its traffic, goes right by the foot of it. Dad told me never to ride down Hill Street on my bicycle."

"Well, you've never really lived until you've sailed down that hill!" exclaimed Warren. "Especially on a sports bike. Like to try it on mine?"

Mark stared at the sports bike admiringly. How ex-

citing to race down Hill Street on it. Quickly, he decided. "OK."

When they got near Hill Street, Warren traded bikes with Mark. Mark remembered his father's warning about the steep hill as he looked down it. But when he felt the new bike under him, the thought of soaring downhill on it overcame all other thoughts. He shoved off and was on his way when Prince joined him. The big collie ran madly behind, trying to keep up.

As he neared the foot of the hill, Mark stamped hard on the brakes. He could see the cars coming and going on Broad Street. Would he be able to slow down enough to turn the corner? The good brakes on the new bike held. Mark sailed safely around the corner.

But Prince . . . Prince kept right on running! Straight out into the traffic he went. There were so many cars there to chase! Mark called, but it was too late. Tires squealed as a car braked, and Prince lay by the side of the road, bleeding.

Mark left the bike and ran over to Prince. Prince lifted his head feebly, then dropped it on the ground —dead! Mark flung his arms around his dog and buried his head in his ruff. "Oh, Prince, Prince," he wailed. "You dumb dog! Why didn't you obey me?"

Suddenly he realized what he had said. Slowly he raised his head. "It was my fault," he muttered. "If I had obeyed Dad, this never would have happened. And I called Prince 'dumb.'" Mark hid his tears in the collie's ruff. "O Lord, forgive me," he sobbed. "And help me square things up with Dad and not be so dumb as to disobey again."

Betty's Shadow

A FICTION STORY by Doris Steinmetz

Betty Wood walked slowly along the dusty city street. She kicked at a can lying on the sidewalk and wished —oh, how hard she wished—that she had a pet— any kind.

Whenever Betty mentioned a pet to her mother, Mrs. Wood said, "Betty, you know we can't afford a pet. Five children are all we can feed on Dad's wages."

Only that morning, Sarah May had come to school bright-eyed. Her dad had bought her a parakeet, cage and all, for her ninth birthday. Sarah May, however, was an only child whereas Betty was the middle one of five.

Betty entered the brown brick building where she lived three floors up. Climbing the stairs, she sniffed the familiar smells of onions and old plaster.

Suddenly she stopped. There on the stair landing sat a big gray cat.

"Mama, Mama, come look!" she called up the stairs.

Mrs. Wood, a tall, tired-looking young woman, appeared at the top of the stairs.

"Look at her, Mama! Whose cat is she?"

"Gracious, girl, I thought something awful was wrong. Why she's a stranger here, just an old alley cat. Shoo! Shoo!" Mother clapped her hands at the animal.

"Mama!" Betty cried. "Why did you scare her? Look at her run! I wish we could keep her."

"Betty, I've told you a dozen times that you can't have a pet."

That evening, Betty slipped out of the apartment after doing dishes. She'd go downstairs and see her grandparents in their basement apartment. Grandpa was caretaker for the building. And Grandma had a goldfish!

As she walked down the stairs, a gray shadow brushed past. The cat! And she had a black rat in her mouth!

"Mama, Mama, come see what the cat has," Betty called. She was sure her mother would be pleased this time. Rats were all around the apartments. Once they had found one right in the baby's playpen!

Mrs. Wood came hurrying out again. "Betty, what—" she began and stopped short when she saw the rat in the cat's mouth. "Why, Dad, come out here and look!" she called.

Dad and the other children crowded around. "Say, that cat's just what we need around here!" exclaimed

Mr. Wood. "Good hunters are hard to find!"

The cat dropped the dead rat and stood, swishing her tail. She looked quite pleased with herself.

"Oh, Daddy, can we keep her?" Betty cried. The

other children danced around happily. Before the cat could run, Betty scooped her up. "I'm going to call her Shadow 'cause she's gray."

After that, Shadow laid a big rat on their doorstep almost every day. The whole family was proud of her. "And to think I tried to run her off," Mrs. Wood said.

One day when Shadow had been missing for a while, Mrs. Wood took Betty down to a basement storeroom. "We've been wondering where Shadow was keeping herself. See what Grandpa found!" There on a dusty shelf on some old rags sat Shadow with five kittens.

"Oh, they're so cute!" Betty exclaimed, reaching out. Shadow hissed and wouldn't let Betty come near. But it wasn't long before she got used to the children playing with the kittens. And finally all but one kitten was spoken for by other families in the building.

A few days later, Betty was visiting Grandma. Grandma was reading to her from her well-worn Bible. Betty glanced out the window and was startled to see the kittens playing in the alley.

She dashed down the hall with Grandma following. But before they could reach the kittens, a strange dog rushed among them barking fiercely.

"Go 'way, you old dog!" Betty screamed. Suddenly there was a flash of gray and Shadow leaped on the dog's back, scratching and clawing.

Startled, the dog forgot the kittens and attacked Shadow. Over and over they rolled, thrashing and snarling. When it was over, Shadow lay dead and the dog slunk off, his head bleeding.

Betty knelt over Shadow's body, crying. Grandma

put her hand on Betty's shoulder. "Don't cry, child," she comforted. "Life is hard at times, but we must be brave. I'm sorry too."

Betty wiped her eyes on her sleeve. "Poor Shadow," she said, sniffing.

"We'd better round up the kittens," Grandma said briskly. "Poor little things must be scared to death."

Reaching under bushes and behind garbage cans, they soon found all five. "Say," Grandma said, holding up a spotted one, "this one isn't spoken for, is it?"

Betty brightened. "No! Oh, maybe we can keep it!"

After they had fed the kittens and put them in their box in the basement, Grandma took Betty into her kitchen for some milk and cookies.

"You know, dear," she said, "there's a lesson in what we've just seen. Shadow didn't have to die, but she loved her kittens and died to save them.

"Remember how I've read to you from the Bible about Jesus? He loved us so much that He died for us too. Only He died to pay for our sins so we wouldn't have to suffer forever in hell.

"You know the Bible says that 'all have sinned' and 'the wages of sin is death.' It also says, 'As many as receive Him, to them gave He power to become the sons [and daughters] of God.' Have you received Him, Betty?"

Betty was silent a minute or two. At last she said quietly, "I think I see it for the first time, Grandma. Jesus loved me and died for me. I'm going to thank Him for taking my sins away right now!"

And she did.

Animal Doctor

A TRUE STORY by Grace Fox Anderson

"All right, Beth, I think we can go and get the cat now," Dr. Robert Allen told his 11-year-old daughter. He led her into a back room or "ward" to get the cat that was going to have an operation.

Ten-year-old Kris waited for them in the operating room. The two girls were spending the morning with their father at Allen Animal Hospital in Broadview, Illinois.

The "ward" was just a small room with several cages of different sizes. Dr. Allen reached into one cage and brought out a pretty, young calico (spotted) cat. He handed it to Beth.

Beth loved cats. This one was a beauty. The fluffy, gold, white, and black cat looked up at her with bright, golden eyes. Beth laughed at the cat's long white whiskers.

"Look, she's wearing a bell on her collar," Kris pointed out when Beth brought her into the operating room.

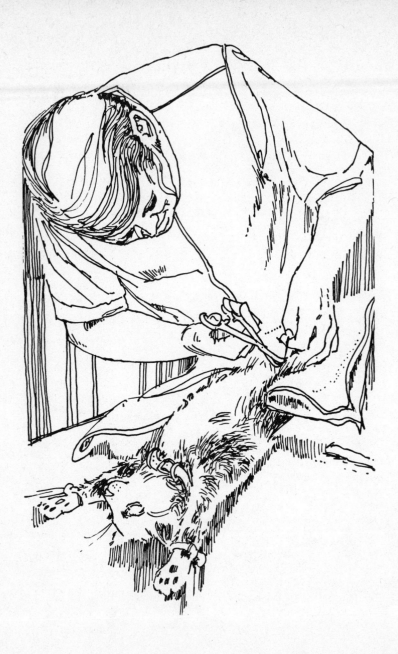

Kris and Beth stroked Miss Cat while their father got the room ready.

Finally he took the cat into his arms and weighed her. "That's so I know how much anesthetic to give her," he told the girls.

"What's wrong with her, Daddy?" Kris asked as he filled his needle with the anesthetic.

"Nothing, Kris. She's in fine condition. This operation will just keep her from having kittens."

At last Dr. Allen was ready with his sterile instruments laid out. The anesthetic was in the needle and his arms and hands were clean.

He applied a tourniquet to the cat's front leg at the top so he could find a vein easily and inserted the needle. Miss Cat was very good. She didn't yowl or scratch. When he'd injected all the fluid, she was sound asleep. Now Dr. Allen had to work quickly.

He turned Miss Cat over on her back and tied her legs down—spread-eagle. Then he shaved off the fur where he would operate.

Taking his scalpel, Dr. Allen first made a quick cut through skin and muscle. Then he took another instrument. With this, he reached inside the cat and pulled out a bit of tissue. He snipped off the tissue and tied the stub. There was almost no bleeding.

Finally, he took his curved needle and "thread" and began the longest process of the operation—sewing her up. He carefully knotted each stitch and cut the thread. This he did several times until the cut or incision was closed.

"I have to stitch her up carefully," he explained, "because she might lick her stitches out if I don't."

"Will it hurt her when she wakes up?" asked Kris.

"Not much," her father answered. "She'll go home tomorrow. She'll get better fast at home."

Dr. Robert S. Allen is a patient, jolly man. He's very gentle with his furred and feathered patients. And he's just as patient and gentle with the animals' owners. His waiting room was full when he finished the cat's operation. But this was the end of Kris' and Beth's visit. Perhaps you'd like to know how their day began.

Before anyone came in to see Dr. Allen, Kris helped her father by sweeping the waiting room. She swept up a lot of animal hair. Then her father mopped the floors and checked on his patients in the "ward."

The first new patient came soon after Dr. Allen's receptionist arrived. The owner brought her dog in, then left quickly. She had brought Pepper, her 14-year-old cocker spaniel, to be put to sleep.

Dr. Allen explained that the dog was sick beyond medical help. "This is the kindest thing I can do for her," he said. Then he showed his girls an ugly cancer on the outside of Pepper's stomach and pointed out that she was losing her sight.

"Pepper was one of my first patients when I opened up my hospital here in Broadview," Dr. Allen told Kris and Beth. "If you multiply 7 times 14, you can figure out about how old she would be if she were a person."

The dog showed no nervousness as Dr. Allen led her into the examining room. He put her up on the table, patted her and talked to her. Then he prepared the needle for the injection that would put Pepper to sleep.

Kris held her leash, but Beth walked out, looking a little teary.

Dr. Allen gently tied Pepper's mouth. Then he started the injection. One minute she was looking up trustingly into the doctor's face. The next minute she plopped over on his examining table—dead. No pain at all. Just as her father was checking Pepper's heart to make sure it was not beating, Beth walked in.

"She's gone to dog heaven, hasn't she, Daddy?" Beth asked, wistfully.

"No, Honey, as far as we know, there's no dog heaven," her father reminded her kindly. "Heaven is just for people who love Jesus."

After checking Pepper over, Dr. Allen picked up her body and carried her out. "A man will come by and pick up the dog's body," he explained.

The girls went out into the waiting room looking sober. They whispered together about Pepper.

Soon other dogs and cats began to arrive with their owners. The door would open and someone would stand there pulling and tugging at a leash. Finally he'd pull his pet inside. Some animals, like a Siamese kitten, were small enough to be carried in. It wasn't long before the waiting room was full. A Brittany spaniel, a silky hound, a Siamese kitten, a big black and white collie, and a schnauzer were all seated with their owners, waiting for Dr. Allen.

Strangely enough, the animals didn't pay much attention to each other. In fact, not one twitched a nose, meowed a meow, or growled a growl. Each animal seemed too worried about himself to care about the others. (According to Dr. Allen, his waiting room is not always so quiet.)

Beth and Kris went into the examining room to watch as each patient was brought in. The spaniel yeowled and yelped though the doctor just checked him over. The hound sat in quiet dignity while her owner and the doctor discussed her problem.

Prince, the big collie, had a rabies shot in his shoulder. When the doctor was done, Prince almost flew out of the room, pulling his young master with him.

Baby Siamese behaved perfectly. She was tiny compared to the collie, but she had a shot too. The doctor also cleaned her ears and checked her all over.

Only dogs and cats were at the hospital that morning but Dr. Allen also treats birds, skunks, raccoons, and other pets. "People bring in skunks and raccoons for rabies shots," Dr. Allen explains.

"I used to work with big farm animals too, but not anymore. One time I was examining a cow's back teeth or throat. A cow's mouth is about 18 inches long. I had my arm in up to my elbow and must have caught my wedding ring on a tooth. The next thing I knew the ring had slipped off my finger and gone 'ploop' right down the cow's throat. So that was the end of my wedding ring." The girls giggle over this story every time they hear it.

The last patient Beth and Kris saw that day was the schnauzer. That's a German terrier with a wiry coat. He had been sick and was being checked again by Dr. Allen.

"Keep giving him the pills. His fever is down but he should have all the medicine just to make sure he's really better," Doctor told the schnauzer's owner.

Then Dr. Allen operated on Miss Cat and the girls' morning visit was over.

Sarah's Adventure

**A TRUE STORY of America in the 1680s
by Grace Helen Davis**

"Ho, Sarah! Thee had better come out and pick up these hickory nuts right by the house! Thee won't want to go into the forest for more, I know." Sarah Owens' teenaged brother, Joel, called to her through the kitchen window in a teasing voice.

"I'll come out when I'm through with my work, if Mother says I may," Sarah replied primly. But a tear almost escaped down her face.

What nine-year-old girl wouldn't be afraid to go into the forest of this new country of Penn's Woods? Sarah had seen a brown bear nearby one day. It hadn't done any harm, but she wouldn't want to meet one while alone in the forest!

And the wolves she heard howling at night scared her even more. The Owens family were Friends, or

Quakers. They had been glad to leave Wales and come to Pennsylvania when William Penn started his colony. Back in Wales they had been badly treated for their religious views.

The Owenses and other Welsh families had settled down just outside the new town of Philadelphia. Father had built a sturdy cottage. He had cut down much of the forest so he could have a good farm. Some trees had been left, though, and one of these was the big hickory by the door.

Pit-pat! Thump! Down the nuts tumbled. Sarah wished she could run out and pick them up. But she was helping Mother make apple butter. Both nuts and apple butter would be needed for the winter.

"Don't thee be bothered by what thy brother says to thee in fun, Sarah," Mother spoke up. "Still, thy father and I wish thee would learn to trust more in the Lord, as our leader, William Penn, doth."

The last of the apple butter was put into a crock. Sarah washed out the big kettle in which it had been boiling. Soon it would be time to start supper. Sarah sighed. It didn't look as though she would be able to run out and gather nuts or enjoy the crisp fall air.

Then Father came in with quick, hurried steps.

"Wife, can thee spare Sarah for a little while?" he asked. "I fear wet weather is coming on. It would be well if Joel and I could get all the corn in this afternoon. I'd be glad if Sarah could go fetch the cows."

"Of course she may, Husband," Mother replied cheerfully. "I can get supper, and the baby has been good. Take off thy apron, Sarah."

Sarah obeyed her mother and started out of the cottage. She wasn't sure, though, that she was glad to go on this errand. Sometimes the cows wandered quite a way!

"Still, I'm just as safe as Joel would be, and I can listen for Beauty's bell," Sarah told herself. "I should trust in the Lord too, as Mother said."

So she hurried along cheerfully and was soon at the edge of the woods. Here was where the cows and Beauty's calf were most likely to be found.

"But I don't hear the cowbell," Sarah said to herself. She climbed on a stump and stared among the trees. There was no sign of cream-colored Beauty or the others.

"Oh, dear, I'll have to go into the forest," Sarah sighed. "Well, at least the sun is shining."

Still she felt nervous as she hurried among the trees. The cows might be in some grassy little glade. Sarah quickly found the spot she knew. But no cows! She went on to another glade, and then remembered a spring.

"Maybe they're still drinking. Coo-bossies! Co-ooo-o, boss!"

No, the cows weren't at the spring, and the sun was setting now. A chill crept into Sarah's heart that matched the chill in the forest air.

"It's getting dark and cold. I'm going to get out and call from the field," Sarah decided fearfully.

She started back, or at least she thought she was starting back. But Sarah couldn't find the clearing of her father's wheat field. She stopped. "I can't be lost!

I know I came this way!" She looked about with growing terror. "How fast the dark is coming!"

Sarah started to run, but a wild grapevine tripped her. Down she went, bruising her knees.

"What will I do? What will I do?" she wailed.

She knew in a moment—pray. Why hadn't she thought to pray before? Sarah knelt down on sore knees and asked the Lord Jesus to help her find her way out of the forest.

When she got up, she took time to look all about her and try to remember where she was. As she stood still, Sarah heard something that made her nearly shout with relief and joy. A tinkling bell! Beauty's cowbell!

"Thank Thee, Lord, for letting me hear it," Sarah whispered, and started toward the tinkles.

"Beauty is leading the other cows home, I'm sure, for she wouldn't go deeper into the woods now."

But as she was stumbling closer to the sound, Sarah heard something else which made her freeze in fear. From far off in the woods came a long, quavering cry —wolves!

"Oh, no! But 'tis—'tis a wolf calling, and another one is answering him!" gasped Sarah.

Beauty must have heard them too, for her bell tinkled loudly and wildly. Then she lowed, "Moo-ooo!" Sarah hurried to find the cow, praying as she went. She soon saw the animals but they stamped and lowed when they saw her.

"It's Sarah!" she called out. The big animals were pleased. Beauty rubbed her neck against Sarah, and Sarah patted her.

"Lead us home, Beauty!" begged the girl.

But just then they heard more far-off wolf calls. Both Sarah and the cows froze. Then Beauty moved forward. Sarah followed along beside her with the calf and other cows.

Beauty led the way to a grassy glade. It was a good-sized one without even a bush.

But instead of passing through the glade, Beauty stopped. In some way she got her plan across to the other cows. They formed a little circle with their heads and horns out, and Beauty's calf and Sarah inside.

Sarah was puzzled and frightened. What were the cows doing? Then she understood. The wolves! The cows had taken a fighting stand instead of trying to get home.

"What will happen?" wondered Sarah. "Well, I must trust Jesus."

It was dark now except for the silvery glint of moonlight through the trees. The cows stood quietly in their ring, their horns lowered.

Wolf calls sounded closer. The cows stamped restlessly. Finally they grew still and tense. Sarah, peering out between them, was sure she saw a pair of red eyes in the forest darkness. Then she saw two pairs. The wolf calls had stopped.

After a time the cows moved and stamped again. Sarah searched for the red eyes but couldn't find them. Then a wolf call quavered some way off.

"They were afraid of ye, kine! They feared those horns!" Sarah cried, and gave thanks to the Lord.

Sarah expected the cows to get into a line again and

start homeward, but they didn't. Instead, the animals kept to their ring, or circle, with lowered horns. Finally, as the wolves didn't come close again, the cows began to lie down one after the other.

Sarah was nearly asleep on her feet, so she lay down beside Beauty's calf, up against the warm bellcow.

The first streaks of light were brightening the skies when Sarah was awakened by her father's voice. "Sarah! Sarah, art thee all right?"

Sarah sat up, feeling cramped.

"Yes, Father! Jesus was with me here in the forest. He told Beauty and the others how to protect me and themselves. I'll always trust Jesus after this, and not be afraid."

This story is based on an account written in a letter from a Quaker woman. She was writing from the new colony of Pennsylvania to her grandmother in England. She tells about a nine-year-old girl out overnight and found peacefully sleeping with the cows in the morning. The letter is found in: Stories of Pennsylvania or School Readings in Pennsylvania History, *by Joseph S. Walton and Martin G. Brumbaugh.*

THE EDITOR

Gary's Guard Dog

A TRUE STORY by Katherine Bradley

It happened the day his mother's friend came to visit from out of town. Ginger set up such a racket barking outside that Gary ran to the door of his mobile home to see what was wrong. There stood Miss Mason, unsure of her next move.

"Ginger won't hurt you, Miss Mason," Gary called to their friend. He went outside and spoke to his ginger-colored cocker spaniel. "Ginger, Miss Mason is our company. You can be nice to her."

Ginger sniffed at Miss Mason's shoes, then wagged her tail.

Miss Mason stooped to pat the wagging pup. "I thought for a minute she'd eat me alive," Miss Mason said, laughing.

"She's a good guard dog," said nine-year-old Gary

Stalcup. "I didn't like being here alone while Mom worked, so I begged until she got me Ginger."

After they had talked a few minutes, Gary took Miss Mason uptown on the bus to meet his mother for lunch. After lunch Gary showed Miss Mason around the stores until his mother finished work. At 4:30 P.M. they all returned to the Stalcup's mobile home by bus.

When they got there, it was strangely quiet.

"Hey, where's Ginger?" Gary cried. "Here, Ginger! Here, Ginger!"

Mrs. Stalcup and Miss Mason called too. But there was no answering bark. Finally Gary's mother said, "I just have to get supper, Gary. Ginger may have followed someone."

The two women went inside but Gary kept calling. Still no Ginger. He leaned against a woodpile to rest a minute and think.

Suddenly, Gary heard a sound like sneezing, coming from under the lumber pile. He got down on his hands and knees and looked under the lumber. There was Ginger, shivering and sneezing!

"Ginger!" he cried. "C'mon, girl. C'mon out."

But she didn't move. Instead, Gary had to crawl in under the lumber and pull her out. "What's the matter, Ginger? Have you caught a cold?" He cradled her in his arms.

Ginger whined faintly and licked his hand.

Gary put his pet down and ran indoors. He got an old piece of blanket and told his mother how he'd found his pet. Gary wrapped the dog in the blanket. Then he sat beside her until his mother called him.

"I'm not hungry," Gary answered.

"Gary, not eating won't help Ginger," his mother tried to persuade him. "She'll probably be all right in the morning."

But Gary would not leave his pet. What if something should happen to Ginger? He remembered how his mother had tried to tell him that God could guard him better than any dog.

"You're a good guard dog," Gary said to Ginger, as if to defend her. "God is mean to let you get sick."

That night Gary did not pray as usual before he got into bed. His mother looked at him anxiously. "Gary, you never miss prayertime. What's wrong?"

"Mother, how could God let Ginger get sick?" he blurted out. "If she dies, I won't have anyone to guard me."

"Gary, I tried to explain before. God will guard you better than Ginger possibly could. God wants to help you if you'll let Him."

But Gary turned to the wall and would not pray.

The next morning he was up early. He warmed milk for Ginger and took it out to her, but she would not touch it.

Gary tried to think of a way he could help his dog. He knew there was no extra money for the veterinarian. Finally he went to his mother. "Mom," he said, "is there any way I can earn money for the vet?"

"If you'll clean up the house this week, I'll pay you what I'd pay Celia," his mother told him. Gary accepted his mother's offer gladly. Celia, a neighbor girl, often came in to help his mother. He knew he could do the things he had seen her do—wash dishes, make beds, scrub the floor.

That week he worked hard and continued to visit Ginger. He had made her a comfortable, dry bed under the woodpile, but the puppy just lay there, suffering. She still wouldn't take the milk he brought.

Finally, at the end of the week, Mrs. Stalcup gave Gary his $5. Gary called the veterinarian right away and explained about Ginger.

"If your dog has never had distemper shots, she may have a bad case of distemper. If so, it's too late for me to help her. You should have called sooner."

"But can't you do anything at all?" Gary pleaded.

"No, Son. But I can put her to sleep for you. When you get ready, let me know. Your pet may live for a couple of months yet."

Gary hung up the phone, stunned. He stared at the money he had worked so hard to earn. He was too late. Ginger was doomed! That evening he told his mother what the vet had said. Then he burst out, "Why did God let this happen to Ginger when I need her to guard me? It will be terribly lonely without her."

"Gary, you're wrong to blame God," his mother explained. "God loves you a lot more than I do. He wouldn't hurt you. Sometimes the things God sends into our lives—even the hard things—can be for our good."

But all Gary could think of was losing Ginger when he needed her as a guard. That night Gary cried himself to sleep as he had when he was a very little boy.

Gary did chores every day that week. Later he would

have the vet help Ginger die kindly with the extra money he was earning.

Ginger seemed to love Gary's visits. Even though she was very weak, she would try to taste the warm milk to please him. And somehow Ginger seemed closer to Gary now than she had ever been before.

One day he said to his pet, "You know, Ginger, if God loves me as much as I love you, maybe He would take care of both of us." Right then Gary decided to pray.

"God, I'm sorry for blaming You for Ginger's sickness," he said. "Please forgive me for not trusting You. If You love me a lot like I love Ginger, please help us both. If it's Your will, please make her well again. But from now on I'll trust You instead of Ginger to guard me."

It was more than a month since Ginger had gotten sick. However, Gary was sure that Ginger began to get well as soon as he started praying. He continued to pray that his pet would get better. And each day Ginger did grow stronger. She began to lap a little warm milk now as if it really tasted good. Finally her nose and eyes stopped running.

One day Ginger struggled out from under the woodpile on wobbly legs. She ate a meal for the first time in weeks. Gary knew then that God had given Ginger back to him.

"Oh, Ginger," he cried, gathering her up in his arms, "God answered prayer for you. Isn't He good! While you were sick, I found out that God can guard us both. I don't need a guard dog, but we can still be pals."

The Bird That Opens Doors

A TRUE STORY by Grace Fox Anderson

Some pet birds open their cage doors. But Teresa is different. She opens house doors.

Teresa, a large blue and gold macaw, has a strong, thick beak. That's what she uses to pry open screen doors.

Her owners, Mr. and Mrs. John Kunkle and their four children, lived in the jungles of Bolivia for nearly 20 years. When they had been there only two years, friends gave them Teresa for Christmas.

She was free to fly around outside most of the time. But she wanted to be inside with the family. So she began letting herself in the house. When the Kunkles hooked the door, she simply chewed her way in. Mr. Kunkle had to make a new door and wrap it in metal.

The Kunkles came home in 1968. They preached the Gospel across the United States and tried to encourage young people to become missionaries. Sometimes they took Teresa with them as they traveled. They discovered that Teresa opens another kind of door—the doors to minds and hearts.

One day, for instance, Mr. (Uncle) Kunkle stopped at a gas station. He returned to the car from the restroom to find an excited attendant.

"Wow," the man said. "Did I get a scare! I was washing your car windows when someone said, 'Hi.' I looked inside the car and there was that huge bird. What in the world is it?"

Uncle Kunkle laughed. "She's a macaw—comes from Bolivia where I've been a missionary."

"A missionary!" exclaimed the man. "Why, you can get killed being a missionary!"

"True," Uncle Kunkle agreed, "but you can get killed quicker on this highway." Then he went on to tell the man about Jesus.

Another time, the Kunkles camped in Yellowstone National Park in Wyoming. It had rained and snowed that night. Two cold, hungry-looking young men were camped nearby.

Uncle Kunkle went over and invited them to eat breakfast with him and his wife. (Their children weren't with them.)

As soon as the young men appeared, Teresa squawked, "Hi."

The fellows laughed and asked about her.

Again, Uncle Kunkle told how he got Teresa.

The fellows asked many questions. They asked about missionary work, the jungle Indians, and Jesus Christ. They were quite impressed with the Kunkles' kindness. Before they all parted, Uncle Kunkle prayed with the two young men.

Again, Teresa had opened the way to talk about Jesus.

Another time, Uncle Kunkle visited a grade school with Teresa. Several boys and girls who saw Teresa at school came later to a nearby church to hear Uncle Kunkle speak. Some of them received Jesus as their Saviour—just because Teresa caught their interest.

Is Teresa friendly? What does she eat? What does she say? How old is she? Uncle Kunkle answers these questions over and over.

He says that Teresa is a bit shy when she first meets people—and may bite. But at times she takes to someone right away.

She's a big bird—about 28 inches long. She was hatched in 1947 and could live to be 80 or 100—longer than her owners.

Teresa eats almost anything people eat, except

candy. She eats meat, potatoes, and fruit. She drinks coffee.

She peels things she eats. She peels fruit, bread, and once peeled a chocolate Uncle Kunkle gave her! She is also a dunker. If food (like bread or cake or crackers) is dry, she flies down to her water dish and drops in the dry food. After letting it soak a while, she eats it.

"Unlike people though," says Uncle Kunkle, "she won't eat anything that isn't good for her. And she won't eat when she's full."

Teresa speaks both Spanish and English. She says, "Dame la pata (give me your foot)" or "Teresa fea (Teresa is ugly)!" She picked up other phrases in Spanish from the school children.

In English she says things like "Polly wants a cracker," "hi," and "pretty bird."

Once, in the jungles, the Kunkles had to punish Teresa for being bad. She was chasing the school children and swooping down and pecking them on the head. She learned to behave after being caged for a few months.

Teresa normally stays outside in warm weather—uncaged. She won't fly away. "Even though other macaws in the jungle tried to get her to join them, she wouldn't leave," Uncle Kunkle says, laughing. "She thinks she's people."

In cold weather, she must be kept warm. Once she was riding in the back of the Kunkles' car. The backseat heater wasn't working and she caught pneumonia. "We prayed for her and I'm sure the Lord touched her, for she got well," Uncle Kunkle tells us.

"We didn't realize what a help Teresa would be when we returned to the States. Sometimes we leave her with friends. But whenever she travels with us, she opens up conversations and people's hearts to hear about our Saviour and the need for missionaries."

We Remember
Baby Robin

**A TRUE STORY told by Mary Sue
and Martha Lou Adair
written by James R. Adair**

It was three summers ago that some children visiting next door found Baby Robin. They called us and we ran to see what they wanted. They pointed to a baby robin on the ground.

Try as he would, the young bird simply couldn't fly. The parent birds cheered him on—and so did we. But it was no use. Baby Robin had tumbled from his nest too soon.

The visiting children went home, leaving us to care for the bird. We couldn't leave him on the ground. A cat might get him. But where could we keep him?

Baby Robin's home became a big box we had painted earlier that week to look like a house. Our friend Jennifer found an old bird's nest, so we put the bird in the box with the nest. Above us, the parent robins scolded excitedly.

Daddy helped us dig earthworms. Mary Sue gently picked up Baby Robin and held him as Martha Lou dangled a juicy worm near his beak. Greedily, he opened wide, stretched, and *gulp!* The worm disappeared down his throat (1).

But our efforts to feed him were not needed. That evening Daddy noticed a movement near the box. A robin (probably the father bird) landed on our picnic table next to the box with food in his beak! Quick as a flash, he flew to the box. He lit on the edge and cocked his head this way and that. Then he disappeared into the box.

When we heard what had happened, we clapped. Our heavenly Father had sent the very best care for Baby Robin—his own parents (2)!

But night was coming, and cats prowl at night. Baby Robin would be in danger!

Daddy solved the problem. He dragged the big red box-house into our garage and closed the door. Baby Robin was safe. But would the parent robins find their baby next morning?

When we woke up, Daddy told us what happened. Only minutes after Baby Robin was outside again, Father Robin swooped down into the box with a beakful of food.

In the days that followed, feedings were frequent.

Like a flash from the sky, a parent bird would come with a worm or some other bit of food. Daddy took pictures from a window. Once a parent bird missed Baby's mouth with a dinner of grubs and a beetle. We fed the food to Baby.

After three days, Baby Robin seemed stronger. His feathers were fuller. He could flutter part way up the side of the box.

On the fourth evening, we discovered him perched unsteadily on the edge of his box.

Next morning, after spending the night in the safety of the garage again, the baby robin flew again to the edge of the box. A few minutes later a parent robin came to feed him.

Then, after Daddy hid in the garage to take pictures, Mother and Father Robin came to coax their baby to fly. Father Robin flew to a telephone line, calling, "Cheerily, cheerily, cheerily!" Soon Baby Robin began answering with a "Squawk! Squawk!"

We went outside before breakfast to say good-bye, for Daddy said he thought Baby Bird was about ready to fly. Mary Sue bent down, pretending to kiss him, and he opened his beak for food (3).

We hid inside the garage with Daddy and watched. The mother kept calling. Baby talked back. We could almost understand: "Now's the time! Spread your wings and try. You can do it!"

"But I'm afraid! I've never flown before. I might fall!"

In a moment of courage, Baby Robin straightened up. Once, twice, three times, he leaned forward.

Mother Robin flew to a lilac bush at the edge of our yard. Baby Robin leaned forward again. He spread his wings and streaked toward her. Daddy clicked his camera a split second after the speckled bird took flight (4).

The last we saw Baby Robin, he flew with his mother from the lilac bush to an apple tree in a neighbor's yard. We called, "Good-bye, Baby Robin. We love you!"

*   *   *

From God's Word: "Take a good look at the wild birds, for they do not sow or reap, or store up food in barns, and yet your heavenly Father keeps on feeding them. Are you not worth more than they? . . . So never worry and say, 'What are we going to have to eat? . . . What are we going to wear?' . . . Your heavenly Father well knows that you need them all. But as your first duty, keep on looking for His standard of doing right, and for His will, and all these things will be yours" (Matt. 6:26, 31, 33, WMS).

Ice Break

A FICTION STORY by Marlene Lefever

Zeke, Mildred's fox terrier, lay in front of the glowing fireplace. His tail thumped as 10-year-old Mildred Keppel jumped up again to look out the frosted window.

Mildred peered fearfully out into the dark night. She looked hard at the frozen Susquehanna River. The river ice surrounding her island home near Lancaster, Pennsylvania was still smooth, except for a depth crack here and there.

"Vell, little one, you must go up to bed now." Her father put his hands on her shoulder and rested his chin on her head. "Your mama and I talked it over. You shall not sit up through the night again. You'll use all the wood. I'll put out the fire and you go to bed."

"Papa, just let me sit up one night more. I know the ice will break tonight," Mildred pleaded.

"Mildred, you've sat up the past three nights because you were certain the ice would break. God will keep us safe."

Mildred realized that Papa knew the river. Her Dutch, Mennonite father had lived much of his 58 years on this little island. The only contact the Keppels had with the mainland came on Sundays when they walked across the ice in the winter or rowed across in the summer to the Mennonite meetinghouse.

Papa could tell when the river would be choppy because of the wind. He also knew, almost to the day, when the Susquehanna would start to freeze and when it would thaw.

Sometimes the ice would break in March. Little piles of ice would build up around the edges of the island. So far the dangerous ice breaks were only experienced in the tales Papa told as truth at the supper table.

He told how the early spring thaws years ago caused big chunks of ice to break apart. These pieces started slowly down the river. Because the water moved faster than the small icebergs, the ice piled into huge drifts. These drifts shifted slowly downstream and crushed everything in their way.

But Mildred was uneasy. Somehow this year, 1897, was different. Papa even said it had been the coldest winter he could remember. Now spring had arrived almost overnight. It had been warm for three days and the ice had melted in its regular way. But because of the fast weather change, Mildred had been afraid the ice would break up quickly, as it had in Papa's tales, and pile many feet into the air.

However, Mildred had stayed up three nights. She had used a lot of wood, and nothing had happened. She bent over and rubbed Zeke's head. Then the two of them headed for the stairs. She looked back to say goodnight to Papa, but his lips were moving silently, and she knew that he was talking to God.

Perhaps he was praying about the ice. He did not seem worried as she was. But surely it would be safer to spend the night with their friends on the mainland! She could not always understand Papa.

It seemed as though Mildred had been sleeping for hours when she awoke. "Get yourself to sleep, dog," she mumbled, aware of some noise. But when she opened her eyes, she saw that Zeke was still sleeping at her feet.

Wide awake, she flew out of bed and to the window. "The ice! The ice! It has broken!" she cried. The dreaded thaw of Papa's stories had come. The ice was piling in some places up the river as high as their house. The water was carrying the ice toward the island. Their small home would be crushed!

"Papa! Papa!" she screamed over the crackling. She rushed to her parents' room. Her father was putting on his shoes. "Get into your shoes, then help your mother, Mildred. We will get ourselves away."

The frightened three gathered in their winter coats and shawls by the front door. The wharf was already crushed under creeping stacks of ice that piled sheet

upon sheet, and shifted downriver by the force of its weight.

"Mama, look! There's a fire on the shore." Mildred pointed to a glimmer of a huge bonfire. She could barely see it through the piles of ice. And it was too far away to see the people, but Mildred guessed that the whole community was on the shore praying for them.

" 'I will guide thee with Mine eye' " Mildred's father whispered.

Yes, God will guide us, I'm sure, she thought.

The family walked down the path. Mama clung tightly to Papa's hand. Mildred just watched the fire and imagined it was God's eye guiding them to safety.

"I can't go out!" her mother cried as they reached the ice. "I can't get over those ice chunks. I won't leave." She ran a few steps back toward the house.

Papa ran after her and held her arms. She sobbed until Papa shook her to make her stop. Zeke ran back and forth toward the barn, barking anxiously. "He vonts to take the cow across," Papa explained to Mama, but Mama only looked out on the ice.

"No, Zeke. Come, dog." Mildred almost smiled at the thought of the fat old cow sliding over the ice. Zeke obeyed and came to her side. They were all at the river's edge now. Without a motion or order, Zeke moved over an ice cake, up to the top and down the other side. Then he returned over the top.

"Not only has God given us the fire eye, but now He's using Zeke's eyes to help us. God will protect us, Mama. I've prayed that He will." The little family held hands as Papa prayed once more that God would be with them.

Then the three—Mildred, Mama, and Papa—started after Zeke in duck fashion over the ice stacks. They would lose sight of the fire as they slid from one mound to the next. Yet back on top, they would set their direction straight again.

They were about halfway across when a deep rumble grew into a roar. Suddenly the solid cake on which they were standing broke in two. A huge wall of ice moved into the space separating Mildred from her parents. At first she thought she heard them calling but then she couldn't tell. "O God," she cried, "help me!"

Even in her terror, Mildred knew she must keep moving. She refused to think about what had happened on the other side of the ice. Soon, over the roar of the breakup, she heard another sound. It was the blare of trumpets and clang of washtubs their friends were pounding to alert them.

She moved slowly up and dangerously fast down. Her hands bled from grasping the sharp ice. Each breath hurt. She felt she could climb no farther. "Guide thee, guide thee, guide thee." Her father's words spoke over and over in her mind.

She had only two more ice hills to cross when she caught sight of her small dog crossing in front of her. He waited until he was certain she was following. His feet must have been frozen, for now he was slipping instead of clawing safely as he had when he started.

The dog led her over the shortest route, down and

up, then a small slide. Finally she could see the faces of those who were waiting. One woman was crying. She ran over a single piece of ice into the arms of a woman she hardly knew. She cried until her sobs caught on her breath.

"Mama?" she asked.

"Vell now, they aren't as young as you. They'll be along any minute."

Mildred strained to see her parents' dark forms. Then she saw something moving. It was Zeke. He was going back for them. It was 10 minutes before the three got near land. Zeke was leading them, as much with his courageous presence as with his keen senses.

Mildred helped support Mama as the ladies covered her with blankets and surrounded her with warm coals. "We thought the Lord had taken you, little one. But your pup must have led you safely across the ice."

Mildred turned and pointed to the fire. "Like a big eye, and God used it and Zeke to bring us safely. 'I will guide thee with My eye,' He promised and He did."

"Yes, and now the four of us are safe." Her father turned to praise the dog. "Where is Zeke?"

Mildred called and then her eyes went to the ice. Just over the second pile, the small dog was struggling to drag himself. He was heading back to the barn.

"Zeke! Zeke! Papa, stop him!" Hot tears burned down her cheeks as she watched her faithful friend head back toward the crushed barn and the ice-mound that used to be their home.

Papa's voice was sad and deep. "He vonts to save the cow too."

Little Lame Chick

A TRUE STORY by Newman Watts

On a cold, bleak day in early March, a wooden crate arrived at our farm home. In the crate were several chicks, just eight weeks old. Dad gave me the job of feeding them.

Two days after their arrival, I noticed one of them being stepped on by the others. I stuck my hand full of feed through the door of the chicken house. The weak chick hobbled over to get some mash. I found out then it was lame.

I carried the chick indoors and showed it to my father. "Well, my boy, here's your chance," Dad said. "See if you can nurse it back to health."

Mary and Audrey, my sisters, wanted to help too. Sisters always do, I discovered. "What shall we name it?" asked Audrey.

"Mephibosheth, of course," Mother answered.

"Yes, Mephibosheth!" Mary shouted. "That's the man who was lame in both his feet." Mary was the oldest and knew a lot more about the Bible than I did. But since she was the only one who could say the word right, we called the little chicken "Mephy."

"I wonder what's the matter with it," I said.

Mother looked at Mephy carefully. "I'm not sure. She may just be sick. The best thing you can do now is keep her warm."

We found a box high enough to keep her from the cold air on the kitchen floor. There we took care of the little lame chick for three days. Then Mary got busy learning a piece for a school program. And little Audrey got tired of stroking Mephy's feathers. So I was left alone to care for the chick.

Soon Mother didn't want Mephy in the kitchen. So I took the box into the toolshed. Mephy learned to eat from my hand. She let me pick her up, stroke her, and stretch her wings. She seemed to like having me around, but she didn't rise up and walk.

When I told Dad, he laughed. "Son, you'll never get her on her legs like that. She'll get spoiled, being hand-fed. You must coax her—make her walk."

So I planned my cure. I put my hand so far from Mephy that she had to struggle to get a peck. Then I helped her on her feet and made her take several steps. Later I put her food in a tin. She had to get up to reach it. She would walk a few steps to get her food, then sit down again between meals.

But I got tired of this. "Mephy," I told her one day,

"you just aren't trying to get better." I decided on a new exercise. Each day I took her to the lawn and, holding onto her tail, I ran her along.

I wasn't very successful at first. Mephy would just sit down. But as the days went by she began to go a little farther. Still, she'd sit down as soon as I left her.

During the time I was working with Mephy, Mr. Harcourt, our minister, gave a sermon one Sunday on "chastening." He said chastening was the same as child-training. "God has to keep making us do something we don't like. That's how He trains us to be more like Jesus," he said.

That's just what I'm doing with Mephy, I thought.

"When we have to do something hard or go through some trouble," the minister continued, "it is a sign that God loves us, and it should make us love Him more."

And you know, that's just how things worked out with Mephy and me. Mephy finally got well, but by then she was special to me. I didn't like the idea of putting her back with the other chickens. She came running to me every time I stepped out the back door. In fact, I had trouble keeping her from under my feet. Mephy and I had become good friends.

Dad finally insisted that I put her in the chicken yard. But the other chicks had forgotten her. They treated her as if she were a stranger. They pecked her so much she would get out of the chicken yard whenever she could.

That's kind of the way the guys at school treat me since I received Jesus, I decided one day as I watched

Mephy being pecked. The guys don't like it because I don't swear or tell dirty jokes.

Another thing I noticed about Mephy: whenever I went into the chicken yard, the other chicks would flutter about as if I was going to hurt them. But Mephy would run up to me to be petted. When I threw scraps into the yard, Mephy never flew around as the others did. She waited for me to drop pieces just for her.

Funny, isn't it? I had never run the other chicks around the lawn, catching hold of their tails. Yet they were afraid of me. But Mephy loved and trusted me.

At last, about October, Mephy and the other chickens began to lay. One day Mother came in with very large eggs. "Mephy was clucking so proudly," she said. "I looked on the nest and sure enough, there was an egg. See, I think it's the biggest yet!"

Yes, Mephy's eggs were bigger than any of the others. It was as if she wanted to say, "I remember all you did for me. So I'll do all I can for you."

The Bible says, "By their fruits you shall know them." And I guess if you judge a chicken by its eggs, Mephy must have been a very good chicken!

With Mephy as my example, I decided that year that I too wanted to bear good "fruit." But mine would be for Jesus. I'd show Him I loved Him by loving others and telling anyone who would listen about how Jesus died so my wrong thoughts and deeds could be forgiven.

After all, I couldn't be outdone by a chicken!

Muff

A TRUE STORY by Marion Bond West

Muff, our 15-year-old dog, lay dying, we were sure.

Usually when my husband Jerry left for work in the morning, I walked out to the car with him. Muff always came wagging out of her doghouse to greet us. But this morning she just lay on her side, her head near the door. She didn't move when I stroked her head. And her old gray eyes looked right through me.

"Well, she is 15," Jerry said, and I nodded sadly. "I'll get off work early and take her to the vet back where we used to live. She won't be afraid of him, and he can put her out of her misery."

Jerry left and I had the task of telling the children about Muff. At almost 16, she was older than any of them. How would they take the sad news?

Julie and Jennifer, 15 and 13, nodded silently as I

told them about Muff. It was harder to tell the seven-year-old twins, Jon and Jeremy.

Jon asked all kinds of questions to relieve his pain. But Jeremy only looked at me for a long time as though he had not understood. The corners of his mouth turned down, and he blinked fast in a brave effort to hold back the tears.

Breakfast uneaten, Jeremy left the kitchen, trying to appear as if nothing were wrong. I heard him flop onto his bed upstairs and followed him up there. He had hidden under his blanket and was sobbing hard.

"Lord," I prayed quickly, "help me not to cry too. I must not while I'm trying to help him. Please show me what to say."

An inner voice spoke silently but powerfully: "Tell him what I'm teaching you about praise."

"But, Lord," I said, "he's such a little boy. It's hard even for me to praise You for everything and I'm nearly 40."

Again the inner voice spoke: "Teach him while he's young to praise Me for all things."

I sat down on the bed and pulled the covers off his head. He looked up at me, his face twisted with grief. I held him close. "Jeremy, will you listen to me carefully for just a minute?"

Still sobbing, he nodded.

"Jeremy, I want you to thank God that Muff isn't going to get well this time," I said quietly.

He jerked away and looked at me, stunned.

"The Bible tells us to thank God for everything," I explained, "not just for the good things. But things we don't like or understand. Even things that may hurt."

He'd stopped crying now and listened closely.

"We've had Muff for 15 years. She's worn out—like a toy Daddy can't fix anymore. We can thank God that she's not lost or hasn't been run over by a car.

"We can thank Him too that Daddy is going to get off work early. He'll drive the 20 miles home then take Muff 40 miles to the vet who knows her. And we can thank God that the vet can help Muff—go to sleep and not wake up. We have to give her up, Jeremy. Let's thank God that He let us have Muff so long."

He bowed his head and said, "Thank You, God, that we had Muff so long. Thank You that Daddy is coming to take her to the vet. Thank You she—can't get well— and is going—to die."

His prayer was so much more than I had hoped for. It was more than I could have managed. To my surprise Jeremy got up, looked in the mirror, and wiped his eyes. He pushed back his hair, tucked in his shirt, and went out to play.

That morning I had an appointment at the beauty shop. I checked on Muff several times before I left home. She was no better. In fact, she looked worse. I watched her sides closely to be sure she was still breathing. They barely moved.

At the shop, my hair dresser asked what was wrong. I told her about Muff. "Oh, our dog got terribly sick the other night," she told me. "He died in agony."

I explained how Muff was acting. "That's just how our dog acted," she said.

Then I knew Muff was not only old and worn out,

she was very ill. Sitting under the hair dryer, I gave up the last bit of hope that Muff might live. Secretly, I had hoped for a miracle. Now I just wanted my husband to get her to the vet before she went through an awful death.

Jerry came home from work early as he had promised. He gently encouraged Muff to get up. But she couldn't. So he carried her to the car, and I opened the door for him. I couldn't watch them drive off.

As I walked back into the house, I said a prayer. If a seven-year-old could thank God that his dog had to die, could I do less? I thanked the Lord that she wouldn't suffer and that Jerry had come home early to take her to our old vet.

After supper, the children went on an outing. I sat alone on the front steps waiting for Jerry. He should have been home two hours ago, I reasoned. What had happened to him? Had he pulled off the road on the way home to get over his grief?

Finally, at 7:20 P.M. our brown station wagon rounded the corner and pulled into the driveway. I strained to see the expression on Jerry's face. He just stared straight ahead.

He got out of the car and walked around to the other side and opened the door. "What is he doing?" I muttered to myself.

Ever so slowly, Muff eased herself out of the car. And she was smiling; I could tell! It was a feeble smile, but she smiled nevertheless and wagged her old tail twice. Then raising her head, she walked unaided to the backyard and her house.

"What happened?" I screamed, as I ran after Muff. I wanted to get to the doghouse before Muff did. I had shut it up permanently and thrown out her water dish.

Muff waited for me to fill a new dish with water. Then she drank a little while. Jerry and I watched. Afterward, she walked slowly around the yard. She stumbled several times and it took her about 30 minutes, but she covered nearly every inch of the ground. Then she returned to her house.

"She didn't have what we thought," Jerry explained. "But she's a mighty sick dog—has worms among other serious things, plus her age." He handed me a bottle. "These pills are for the worms. Give them to her in four days. She's too sick to have them now."

"What did the vet do?" I demanded.

"He put fluids into her veins and gave her a big dose of penicillin," he answered.

Muff made amazing progress. In four days, she was galloping around the yard again, even barking. She ate like a wolf and wagged her tail at all of us. Her coat became shiny and she began to act like a puppy.

The children had screamed and hugged her when they came home and found her in the yard. But before Jeremy hugged her, he said, "Now we need to thank God for letting her live, don't we?"

"We certainly do, Jeremy," I agreed. And I thanked God silently—not only for sparing Muff's life but also that our family was learning to praise the Lord for ALL things.

Hungry Lions

A TRUE STORY by Marilyn Eck

Lions, lions, lions!

The Marvin Ecks were missionaries in Africa. They lived near the Nile River and often saw lions.

Sometimes they heard reports of lions killing animals belonging to African villagers. A hungry lion had even been known to attack a human being.

These kings of beasts were especially active at night.

One day Mr. Eck left home to build a new mission station. He traveled by cart about 18 miles inland to the new site near the village of Paloich.

There he set up camp and began building. Days, he worked hard. He hired some Africans to help make bricks of mud and grass.

Nights, the Africans went back to their village, but

they would not let Mr. Eck stay with them. Instead, he slept alone on a cot out under the stars. His only covering was a mosquito net.

One evening before he went to bed he heard lions roaring. As usual he was alone—no gun, no shelter. He remembered how God had protected Daniel in the lions' den. Now he prayed that God would protect him too.

The roaring came closer.

"David killed a lion with his bare hands. Perhaps God will give me strength to do that tonight," Mr. Eck thought. By this time he could hear several lions coming his way. "If only the natives weren't so superstitious, I could sleep in the village," he said half aloud.

The lions were coming closer and closer. They sounded hungry. Mr. Eck lifted his head to see how close they were. Though a full moon bathed the countryside, he could not yet see them.

Suddenly a gleam caught his eye. There lay his hatchet. (He always kept it handy beside his shoes just in case a snake or scorpion decided to stay in one until morning.) Quickly he opened his mosquito net to reach out and pick up the hatchet.

"You said your hope was in Me," a small voice seemed to whisper.

"Yes, Lord, it is. But just in case one of those lions comes too close, I can knock him out," was Mr. Eck's quick reply.

"Can't you trust Me completely?" the voice seemed to plead.

"Of course I can, Lord. Forgive me for my lack of faith. My hope is in Thee." Mr. Eck dropped the hatchet. He realized again that God really could do all things. He realized that this was a time when God was asking him to "stand still, and see the salvation of the Lord."

Now, in the bright moonlight he saw three beautiful lions. One was a large male with a big shaggy mane. Just behind him walked the sleek female with a cub trailing at her heels. They sniffed at the pile of mud bricks. They sniffed at the buckets used for carrying mud. Then—they walked straight to the mosquito net.

Mr. Eck lay perfectly still. He must trust the Lord to keep his heart from pounding loudly and frightening the lions.

Each lion sniffed the mosquito net in turn. Then each one shook himself and walked away. They were disgusted with the smell of the white man!

"Great is Thy faithfulness, O God, my Father." Mr. Eck's heart praised the Lord even while he remained quiet on his cot.

The next morning as the boys came out of the village they told him that some lions had broken into a sheep barn and killed 13 sheep.

I'll always be thankful that God so wonderfully protected Mr. Marvin Eck. For you see, he was my father.